GUSTAV'S TRAVELS

D. S. LINDBERG

TABLE OF CONTENTS

I'm thankful to the group of ladies who invited everyone in the company I worked for to participate in creating pumpkin decorations. I'm not very artistic, but I thought that socializing was a good trait. We were given these small pumpkins to decorate. I drew a small face upon one that I had received and placed it on my desk and left it alone.

After a day or so, I felt more artistic and took the silly thing home to improve. I decided to put this on a small carriage and give it a different appearance. I spray painted the carriage black and gold. I devised a small set from a box top with a scene of rolling hills and a castle in the background. The next day, I brought this beautiful setting to work and set it next to the other entries. Of course, the other pumpkins were all dressed up in dresses and pretty hats. You know who won that contest. They were all very pretty, and I'm sure the decision was difficult; my little pumpkin carriage seemed out of place and alone. I took it home, defeated.

This is now part of our decorations for Halloween at home. The more I looked at this set, the more I felt that there was an untold story within the orange orb. When I first wrote about Gustav, the set is what gave me inspiration. The evolution of the story was slow and frustrating. When I wrote the basic story, I felt it was a long short story. How little we know of man's imagination. It is a strange evolution, as Gustav, the pumpkin seed, Gretchen, Ariel, and others continue to grow the story line.

These first episodes of Gustav with his several adventures were kind of laid to rest as I put the manuscript aside. I had submitted the idea to several publishers and was turned down. Then, just a few months ago, here in the year 2013, I discovered a voice-recognition software that has overcome the shaky hands of an almost seventy-year-old man. What a joy it has been to re-create and flesh out this story. Hopefully, it will be published and finished before I am. Thank you, Gustav, and all the others of the cast.

CHAPTER ONE

FARMER TO KNIGHT OF THE REALM

The rolling hills and plains of the Valley were embraced by majestic granite and limestone peaks. There were several passages that led in and out of this jewel of a valley. Well-worn pathways were actually ancient roadways allowing travelers and merchants entrance into the Valley. Anyone approaching these two narrow passes would be greeted by large stone gates with accompanying watchtowers above the roadways. These gateways each had modest living quarters for members of the king's militia, men who had enlisted for a certain time to be part of this home guard. There were the first lines of defense for the Valley. If a large force of unknown intentions was seen approaching the passes, an alarm would be sounded that could be heard from the fortress. Within hours, additional forces would be sent to the pass that sent the alarm.

Above each of these narrow passes was a protection of last resort. This was a rockfall that could be triggered to temporarily block the pass. Since both passes had large boulders throughout, the militia had been able to create the rockfall. There was a large boulder above each pass that had been undercut and blocked, so that with little effort, one could cause the rockfall. The only catch to this protection was that whoever dislodged the rockfall better be a good runner.

There was also a cadre of seasoned veterans taking part as officers and administrative personnel. This was not an army of belligerence, but protectors of the borders and of the realm. They also provided a first defense against intruders, robbers, and bands of wanderers. The merchants who traveled into the Valley brought goods for sale and bought trade items that were crafted by many tradesmen who lived in this land. Surplus foodstuffs were also bought and sold. On certain days of the week, people of the realm were allowed to speak with the king and his advisors. There were small cooking fires preparing certain delicacies; the aromas were a pleasant addition to the festive air within the market. The king's guard patrols the grounds to ensure that all went well. It was a very busy place that reflected the better times within the valley of Angus.

As you entered the valley, you would see rich farmlands, some with fields of wheat, oats, and rye that appeared as gold and white rolling seas of sustenance. As one would look to one side of the valley, you would notice a large fortress. This large stone edifice was as a massive throne against the largest of the granite peaks. This building was known as Castle Angus. Created from native stone and mortar, it stood as a monument to the early settlers of the valley. To the front of the castle could be found stables, storage buildings, and many smaller buildings where merchants could display their wares. This large open area was surrounded by a massive wall.

The outer wall had walkways along the interior where members of the militia could keep watch over the Valley and those who entered the large open area in front of the castle. To provide the funds needed to maintain the army and upkeep of the realm, there was a tax on goods and services. This tax, as with in any land, could be a cause of contention. But there could be resolution, and in this valley there was: it was the king and his advisors.

Many years before, a wise king and his advisors knew they must be part of this land if the land were to flourish. Though a monarch, the king relied upon advisors who represented the people. Yes, the king had his riches, resplendent clothes, and a queen whom he adored, but the kingdom came first. He knew many of his people by their first names, and he knew their children. The king and queen had a son who was destined to be the next monarch. Their son was the commanding general of the militia and worked tirelessly at improving this force of veterans and civilians.

As the harvest continued throughout the Valley, so also were many young men and one woman who were preparing for the fall enlistment games. They were called games, though in actuality these were tests of ability, strength, stamina, and courage. As it was for many years, this was a time for some of the so-called "old guard" to retire.

The King and his Queen stood looking out over this grand land, the king lamented, "I wonder what the games will bring in for our militia."

The queen stood next to her mate and wrapped her arm around his waist. Looking up into his chiseled face, she felt an involuntary shiver. "Are you chilled, my king?" He took a long deep sigh and then gazed into her beautiful face and said, "There are so many changes in the outside world, I am puzzled by some of the folks who have sought refuge in our land." She looked out, observing the comings and goings of soldiers walking their post. Then the queen watched merchants and craftsmen as they closed their shops and stalls. Looking back to her mate, she asked, "To what folks do you refer?" He spoke in a low whisper, as visitors were leaving and the great doors closed, "Oh, there is an occasional odd person or two. The oddest of all is this woman and her cat." "Cat, you say? I haven't seen her. Should I watch for her?" asked the queen.

He spoke slowly. "No, Margaret, do not seek her out. Many believe that she is a sorceress. Her powers are not known in this land, but word from other lands is that one must stay away from this lady and her beast. I have seen this cat. I fear for our little ones and the small creatures that roam free. The beast is larger than any of the four-legged creatures in our castle, except for the horses and cattle. I believe that even a good-sized man would have a terrible battle to survive." Suddenly, a large screech echoed through the Valley.

"The beast sounds hungry," said the monarch. With this, the king escorted his queen back into their residence. Throughout the valley, worried parents called for their children. The darkness of the night brought a deathly still to the land. All who slept would suddenly awaken in the night wondering if they will be protected.

Angus, great-great-grandson of Angus I, closed the door to their residence. After a brief time, the queen, Margaret, found her mate reclining on their bed. He had lain there for a while, propped up on several large down-filled pillows. He motioned to her and said, "Come, lay with me." She sat in front of the mirror, combing her long brown locks and, turning to him, asked, "Will you protect me?" With a mischievous grin, he said, "Always, my dear." She went to his side and they embraced.

Their love was strong, and sustained them all through the years of his monarchy. Her advice was always helpful, her passion always needed.

As the morning light caressed the peaks in hues of gold, sounds of life began to echo around the fortress and through the Valley. Tradesmen began arriving at the castle gate so they could open their stores and stalls within the castle walls. Farmers continued the harvest, and there was excitement in the air. Many a young man or woman practiced their fighting skills in preparation for the weeklong event of choosing new militiamen.

The sounds of the night were lost in the daily activities of life. From the walls of the castle, a lone sentry brought a strange brass instrument to his lips and sounded a plaintive call, announcing the opening of the great doors. The massive oak gates were slowly pushed open by a squad of men. Because of the size and weight of these doors, it took a great effort to open.

High on the wall and at one corner of the inner walkway, two soldiers could be seen conversing. "Did you see the lady and her beast, Nathaniel?" "Aye, lad, the beast appeared hungry, and when it looked into my eyes, I felt as its prey. Nothing cleared a path through a crowd of people faster than that sorceress holding the long chain attached to that cat. What an animal, larger than any of our hounds, as long as a standing man, with that beautiful long gray pelt with black strips. I think most of us just about watered our trousers when it lets out that roar.

"Fortunately, the great cat and her mistress left this place after making their presence known yesterday. I think they reside in a large tent on the other side of the valley. Maybe she'll tire of this land and find others to frighten, or feed upon. It is thought to feed at night." As the two soldiers gazed into the distance, another soldier quietly walked behind them and said, "Boo." Both of them turned and quickly came to attention, facing the captain of the guard.

"It's a lovely day for daydreaming, is it not?" The older of the two quickly remarked, "No, sir. Just keeping a lookout." "Return to your duties," said the captain. Then, after inspecting each man closely, he commanded in a slowly increasing crescendo, "Let's get back to work, and let us not worry about the big kitty and its owner." They both saluted and returned to their walking posts along the fortress walls.

The captain looked out and said to himself, "Yes, strange woman and hungry cat, what are you up to?" As the captain turned, he looked across the courtyard and noticed that the king and queen were standing high above at the balcony rail. He straightened up, threw back his shoulders, and looked up to them. Their eyes met, and he saluted. He silently mouthed the words, "Good morning, Father." The king winked and returned his son's salute. After returning the salute, the captain of the guard continued on his way, checking all of his posts.

Located within the surrounding walls were storage rooms that held grains and other commodities that could help if under siege. The fortress was to be a haven for those in the Valley who sought refuge from marauders. Within its walls were the king's residence, the residence for the captain of the guard with his family, and the residence for the king's elite; and on the main floor was the grand hall where the king met with his people. There was a natural free-running spring located deep within the bowels of the fortress that provided water for all its inhabitants. It was thought by the inhabitants of this great edifice that the Castle Angus was impregnable. But the enemy comes in all shapes and sizes, as this people will find; sometimes it enters when you least expect it.

CHAPTER TWO

LOVE MATCH

Throughout the Valley, one could find young men and women who were waiting for the call to attend the games. There were many retired militiamen who owned farms. One such farm could be found several miles away from the fortress. There, you can find numerous fields of grain surrounding a modest home and a large barn. This day, one could hear what appeared to be small battle occurring unseen behind a barn.

Found in this secluded area were two individuals locked in a duel. One combatant was a young man with well-muscled body and long blond hair. He had taken off his shirt and was sweating profusely. He demonstrated great skill as he fought his hooded opponent of matching skill. The shirtless young swordsman called out to his opponent, "I will prove myself this year. It is my time to win. This year I will become a militiaman as my father before me. He has led the way, and I will continue to lead. You, my friend, will be my first conquest."

Laughing, his opponent called out to him in a sweet soprano voice. "Don't get so caught up with yourself, my young friend and lover." With that, she issued a challenging insult with a glancing saber slap to the young man's bottom. "Serious mistake, my friend!" he shouted and then saluted his opponent. They began a brief dance of circling each other and touching the tips of their swords. He began a series of attacks to weaken his opponent's defenses. The shirtless young swordsman, with well-practiced skill, drove his hooded opponent to the outer wall of the barn. His fencing partner fought vigorously but was finally pinned to the wall, and she called for quarter. "The match is yours, but the battle is undecided, dear Gustav." "Ah yes, the battle, my dear." With that, he quickly pulled back the other's hood and kissed his lovely betrothed passionately on the lips.

Then she spoke again in her seductive soprano voice. "Ah, Gustav, my love, I do not concede this match to such an unfair diversion." This said by the young girl with flowing locks of auburn hair, dancing sapphire eyes, and the tip of her sword touching center his chest. He moved back, calling out in great surprise: "A devious move, my love, and subtle like the sweet essence of your kiss." He then blew her a kiss. "Words to sway and distract me off my guard, dear love?" said she. "Please keep moving back as I consider your fate."

He moved back cautiously over the uneven ground and tried to remember where the pond was located. Too late, he suddenly called out, "Ariel!" shouting her name as he fell back into the cold muddy water of the pond. The young maiden laughed with gusto as the geese honked and ducks noisily exited; and the young man, soaked to the skin, looked up to his lovely opponent. Quietly, she placed her sword down upon the soft earth. She began shaking her head back and forth, giggling. With a strange, wicked smile, she took off her hooded cloak and just stood for a moment. What a beauty she was as she stood there laughing. Her sweet lips curled in an innocent, cherubic grin. The simple farm dress she wore appeared as a gown which accentuated her young form in just the right places. He smiled, and then he looked at her quizzically. She nodded her head; and her face, though radiant, changed to a very serious expression, almost a frown. The young buxom woman then began to run toward the pond and her love.

He called out to her, suddenly realizing what she was doing. "No, no, you're not going to do what I think you're going to do, are you?" "You don't know me very well, my love." This said, she ran toward the pond, her face showing a wicked smile. She ran quickly the short distance and, with her arms outstretched, dove, hitting the pond with a terrific spray of brown, muddy water. As she landed next to her opponent, he was totally saturated, and so was she. Rolling over, she sat up quickly and embraced him.

Just then, they both saw a horseman entering the farmyard. He noticed the two in the pond, and curious, he rode toward the pond and the two soaked lovers. They quickly exited the pond as best they could, for they noticed that he was a guardsman of the king.

An act of futility, standing before a knight of the realm. They appeared as two very wet lovers.

The horseman tried to suppress a laugh and maintain his composure. The king's knight sat up straight on his mount and announced his intention. "I seek William Gustav, applicant to the king's elite." "I am he, noble sir." Gustav made a serious effort to stand straight and tall as he responded. He was mocked in his effort as the waters of the pond flowed freely from his long hair and very wet clothing. He saluted the knight and waited for a response. The horseman finally succumbed to a fit of laughter and called out, "Now that I have witnessed your baptism, the king wishes your presence for the games. I recommend another bath and clean clothing. You are requested to be there in three days. We will meet at sunrise on the castle grounds." With a spirited salute, he turned his mount and galloped out through an open gate and onto the country path. His laughter echoed over the fields until he was out of sight.

As the two young lovers embraced and watched the horseman leave, a cool breeze caused them both to shiver as they held each other tightly. They looked lovingly into each other's face. Gustav reached and held her face gently with his strong hands and passionately kissed her lips. As they stood there shivering, they savored this quiet moment. Then she said with a plaintive note, "Please, Gustav, give me your promise that you will return to me, no matter your condition or how long it may have been since we last met." "Center my heart is pierced by your sweetness and love. I most certainly will return to you, always," this said by the knight to be. The shadows of the evening began to spread upon the land; he found her cloak and slowly enveloped her in its warmth. He then walked her home, which was a short walk away. It was a long and thoughtful journey back to his home. He found time later in the evening to talk to his parents of the challenging news.

His father had returned from the fields and, after cleaning up, sat with his wife and son at the family table. There they ate a simple broth and homemade bread. Gustav couldn't stop talking in his excitement in response to the call. His father cautioned him, "My son, you're a gentleman, and there are many out there who will take advantage of your good nature. You must be wary of any hidden dangers. Trust your friends, keep them close, but know your enemies." "I thank you, Father, for your concern.

I have learned much from you and my many opponents. I have especially learned from my love. She is an expert swordsman, and she does not let me rest my guard. I have the wounds to prove it," he said as he absentmindedly began rubbing a sore spot. His father smiled and nodded. "There aren't many youngsters who learn such lessons from childhood sweethearts. Ariel is a jewel, and you must protect her and learn from her. Her mind and spirit soar. I hope you've learned to fly."

"Such eloquence from my father?" said Gustav. "She will be my first daughter," said the senior. "You could not have found a finer prize in hunting the four corners of this world." "Pride from my shy and humble husband?" his mother exclaimed as she embraced her husband. He patted her rump with a gentle slap, and she let out a squeal. "Mock me not, woman, she'll be your daughter too." His wife laughed. "Ah, so she will, my love." She stood there, looking at him with her hands on hips saying, "You will then have two women to lead you around the farm like an old bull."

Gustav laughed as he looked to his mother and father. "I need to finish my chores. Wish me luck for tomorrow. I am a swordsman also because of your lively repartee." As their young son walked away, his mother leaned over and whispered to her husband, "I fear for his safety and his life." His father simply nodded his head and stared out toward his son. Little did he know what his son was going to face, but he knew his son was ready for anything. Later, his dad found him as he finished his chores. He bid him sit and talk. "This may be the last time I speak to you before you join the militia. I know I haven't been the easiest person to know, but please rest assured that I'm very proud of you and I believe in your success. Promise me that you will always find your mother during your travels. Gustav looked to his father, saying, "Wherever I am, the evening winds will speak, and you will feel my presence and hear my voice."

CHAPTER THREE

THE GAMES BEGIN

Three days later, in the dawn of a cold dark morning, all the candidates stood before their king as he watched from his balcony. The candidates represented all walks of life within the Valley. There were farmers, merchants, and a few ne'er-do-wells. One striking individual who stood out among them was a young woman. She was known to be as good as swordsman as any within their ranks. Surrounding these young aspirants were members of the king's cadre. These were the seasoned veterans of the militia who were already watching, testing, and observing this new crop of candidates. They were observing for skill, attitude, correctness in the court, and that special presence that would set them apart from the common folk.

The king stood tall in his regalia as he observed the candidates. The queen stood to his side in resplendent beauty. There were stands located along side the outer walls of the fortress that allowed visitors a vantage point to observe the trials. The captain of the guard ordered the candidates to face the king and queen, and then they saluted. The crowd cheered as the games officially began.

The games were actually organized into stations, wherein the candidates were paired off. The stations had various tests, such as archery, throwing the javelin, physical fitness, and finally, combat with the sword. There were cadre members at each station to judge and pick the best. Several candidates did not make it past the first contest. These candidates were either out of shape or had no skill. The call to the militia was a strong desire for many within the Valley to find purpose and maybe just impress king. Some were just hungry for a dangerous change in their lives.

Throughout the coming days, their numbers decreased as there were winners and losers. A few of those who may have lost were encouraged by the cadre to increase their skill level and try again at the next call. There was a carnival atmosphere as the crowds cheered, families cried and cheered again. There were also vendors selling dried meats and sweet nectar. Within just a couple of days, their numbers have been reduced to only four candidates. The crowd was the largest in years, as many came to see the young woman soldier of fortune.

Gustav was one of the four remaining candidates. The young woman had survived numerous battles disguised as a man. Today, she stood as a woman warrior, who had proven herself to be a worthy opponent. Her body armor shone with meticulous care. Her helmet was striking in its detail, for the visor's face was a woman's, with a slot in the rear of the helmet to accommodate her long braid. Her weapons included a razor-sharp sword and tall bow with a quiver full of deadly arrows. The king whispered to his mate, "Those young men are going to have a battle royale trying to best that beautiful warrior." His queen playfully countered, "Just keep your eyes on the match, my love." He cheerfully embraced her, saying, "Yes, my queen, the match." He continued to whisper, "Here's to the best contestant." The final matches began with the sword, since all four of the candidates had matched each other in archery, decorum, and appearance.

The woman paired off with a dashing fellow who came from a wealthy family. This young man had been prepared by several of the king's advisors. His body armor was bright with newness, but his sword, a family heirloom, was well used. He demonstrated a very sure, almost cocky, presence as he saluted his large cheering section. He was seen blowing kisses to his many female admirers and appeared to strut his way around the grounds. He smiled and saluted the female warrior, who chose to stand quietly and observe the somewhat pompous young man. Gustav, on the other hand, was facing the son of a militiaman who demonstrated a very strong yet subdued charisma. As he appeared to warm-up, his swordplay with a shadow opponent demonstrated the man as a very self-assured swordsman. The young fellow saluted his father, who stood in the gallery in his full dress uniform.

Since there was now room in the courtyard for both contests, the matches would be held simultaneously at opposite ends of the open area. This was Gustav's first attempt at the games, so he appeared nervous, even anxious, as he watched the others. His father motioned him over for a quick pep talk. "Look at me, boy. You are as good as anyone here. You have advanced because of your skills, you have made your mother and I very proud. Enjoy this contest and win. You will win. Join with that rowdy bunch of onlookers. They will feed your energy from their cheering."

He looked into the eyes of his father and nodded and saluted both of his parents. He then walked to the center of the grounds. The onlookers cheered from all over castle grounds. The guards were present and at their posts, yet they could be seen cheering. Finally, the two matches ended. Showing extraordinary skill, the young woman won her match. Gustav also won. Now there were two contestants left to determine the winner. Gustav and the young lady faced each other. The captain of the guard called for a brief recess to drink and renew.

There was a great roar of the approval as Gretchen raised her sword and greeted the crowd. Stately in her armor, she stood and turned, taking in the moment. She turned to Gustav and bowed slightly and then gave a slight smile. He smiled in reply and turned to raise his sword for approval. The crowd roared and cheered him also. He walked over to Ariel, as she stood in the stands with his parents. He continued to respond to the crowd. Ariel pulled him close, kissed him gently, and whispered, "Wipe that smirk off your face, my love, the wench is as good as or better than you, and her only desire is run you through. I believe she is hungrier than you."

"You are a great help, woman. You've taught me many moves and also helped me overcome many weaknesses, and then you tell me this?" Ariel whispered, "Just treat her as an adversary, and don't be such a gentleman. Give that woman any break, and she'll take advantage of you. If you lose, I'll be hearing 'only ifs' for years to come. Remember, you will not lose." Reaching over to her love, she nibbled on his ear. "Please, not here, not now." This whispered by the young candidate, Gustav. The crowd hooted, laughed, and roared its approval of the lovebirds. There was a call to order as both contestants were motioned to the center of the courtyard by the captain of the guard. The final contest was about to begin. The young woman was strikingly beautiful, with her long hair tightly drawn into a single braid. She had taken off her helmet and watched her opponent as he spoke and wrestled with the young lady, who appeared more to be more than a friend. She has studied combat with her uncle, who was a retired militiaman. She had studied in secret until her family found out about her personal desire for combat. They threw her out of her home of birth. Since then, she lived by her wits and skills as a soldier of fortune.

She had been in battles in other lands. These had tempered her abilities, as heat to a fine sword. This now was a chance to add to her credibility and to become a woman in the king's elite. It would be a personal achievement, a victory, and hopefully a new home. As a final match was announced, the crowd hushed, and all waited for the beginning. Although evenly matched in height, weight, and age, Gustav appeared awkward in his youthfulness. But his appearance was deceiving. If you looked carefully into his eyes, you may have seen a determination that could overcome many weaknesses. The young woman, on the other hand, had learned to shield her emotions. She appeared focused and emotionless, almost stern. She was ready.

Turning to the crowd, the woman realized she had no family to cheer her, so she found a man and woman who just happened to be Gustav's father and mother. She imagined them as her parents. Calling to them, she raised her saber in salute. "For you, your honor, my blood. I am your daughter and will always be so." The senior Gustav heard with his wife this grand salute from his son's opponent. Not wishing to break the spell, he bowed and called to her above the roar of the crowd, "You make us proud, my dear, carry on." Then they waved to both contestants.

The woman was taken aback by the courtesy shown by the couple. She bowed slightly and mouthed the words "Thank you." Gustav had observed this small play within a play, and when his eyes met his parents, he looked at them with a questioning glance. They smiled, and his dad saluted him. Then the two were called to the center. The two swordsmen bowed and touched sword points, and the final game began.

CHAPTER FOUR

VICTORY

After a few thrusts and parries, the combat became real, and the field of battle began to expand. Gretchen and Gustav began to look for weaknesses in the other. The order of battle changed by the moment as quick thrusts and attacks by Gretchen would push Gustav back. Then, just as quickly, he would change the direction, with Gretchen being forced back. This seesaw battle continued for minutes at a time, as the contest became so intense that there were cheers as each swordsman seem to pull out in one more block or parry. There are many superficial cuts and marks of touché on the man and woman as they began to tire and make mistakes. They appeared as though dancing a very dangerous waltz of death. As they moved from one end of the courtyard to the other, one of them would be forced atop a table or into a booth, which made the dance even more dangerous.

As Ariel watched, she had to stifle a scream each time there was a close jab at her love. She cheered until her voice was hoarse; her body moved in tandem with Gustav as he appeared to be fighting for his life. Finally, some would say a fluke, some would say a plan, Gustav moved back in defense and appeared to slip and fall back, with his sword thrown high in the air. Gretchen lunged forward to mark touché, but he blocked it with his arm, receiving a slash from her saber. There was an audible gasp from the crowd as his weapon fell back into his hand, and he touched her center with the tip of his sword. "Yield!" he shouted.

She closed her eyes and realized what had happened. She looked into his face and nodded slightly. He returned that nod, and they both stood.

There was a tumultuous roar from the crowd, and then just as quickly, they quieted. Gretchen was surprised and unharmed as she realized that victory was not hers today. There were cheers and a few scattered boos, as some questioned the final outcome. She was also a woman of honor, as she bowed to the monarch and pointed to her opponent. "My king, I give thee a new member of the elite."

There were shouts of approval, and many were dancing in the courtyard in celebration. Finally, the king allowed for a few more moments of celebration, and then he called for quiet. He was now on the grounds of the courtyard as he asked for both contestants to come to him. He then called out, "Such a day for gentlemen and ladies to witness. We are blessed in this Valley and rewarded this day with a show of remarkable skill and, most of all, honor. Young Gustav and Mistress Gretchen, we are honored, and I salute you both. Gustav, you will be a new member of my elite. Gretchen, you're not without honor. For such a remarkable demonstration of skill and honor, I will create a new position. You will become an assistant master at arms and candidate in waiting. You will be training, and when a new position is opened and posted, it will be yours."

With an uncharacteristic grin, the young woman bowed and saluted her opponent. Surprising everyone, she walked over to Gustav and embraced him. Whispering in his ear, she said, "Thanks for giving me no quarter, my friend." She then turned and faced Ariel and saluted her with a wink. She was surprised as her stage parents walked through the crowd and embraced them both. She now had a new set of parents and maybe a brother. What a cause for celebration as the king and his realm enjoyed the day.

In the months following this contest, Gustav could be found learning close-order drill, tactics, and other military skills. He also learned formalities of the court. Gretchen also received the same instructions. She learned duties of the court, and as with all militia, combat with the sword was a constant drill. The king had covered Gretchen's expenses by assigning her extra duties in the court. In time, this move pleased the keeper of the treasury.

One of the minor nobles of the court made the mistake one morning of commenting about the only woman in the elite. He was heard to say, "How absurd, a common housemaid, now a swordsman for the king." He had not noticed the king, who had entered and listened.

The speaker was greatly alarmed as the king spoke behind him. He turned and bowed to the king. "Please, sir, find the wench, reassign her, and take her place in all the many assignments she handles through the day and late into the evening. You may do these seven days a week, with one hour off the prayer on Sunday."

Then, stepping up to the cowering nobleman, he whispered in his ear, "Be also ready for the weak-kneed backstabbers that lie in wait." The king, not being one to show anger, simply walked away to his throne. He then sat, folded his arms, and smiled as the repentant noblemen exited the court. The cowardly minion was seen almost crawling through the door. As he left, there was a great and thunderous applause, as all who witnessed this event knew the King and loved him for his forthright manner of dealing with his people.

CHAPTER FIVE

THE SORCERESS AND THE KING

Gustav was assigned a rotating basis to posts within and outside of the castle. One day, Gustav was assigned with a number of his fellows to the court of the king. They were there to keep order and to protect him. Gretchen was assigned to assist petitioners and their pleas to the king. Since many of the petitioners were simple folk, the help that she offered brought about a change to the number of people seen. This too pleased the monarch. She was also inducted into the king cadre's as the first female to guard Angus, with the exception of the queen. Times were good; the king's enemies were few, and the country prospered. But there came the day that changed life within the militia and affected all, even the king.

Monday had arrived, and all were recovering from a slow weekend. Gustav found reason to scuffle with anyone. He had just practiced the saber with Gretchen and barely won after a long dry spell of losing to her. The large brass doors leading to the great hall were opened. These audiences with the king provided opportunity to meet with him. They are giving hearing for them who sought reevaluation of taxes, forgiveness of debt, or the settling of disputes.

Gretchen moved over to Gustav and whispered, "That lady, the sorceress, has arrived with her cat. Be aware." Into the large chamber came the sorceress, holding on to a long silver chain attached to a large cat. No one within the kingdom had made their presence as well-known as this woman. Her name was Barbarossa. Such a name for woman, it was a type of wild boar that was found in a distant land. The animal was known for its evil temperament. She lived up to of that image. She was very tall, a big boned lady who many thought to be quite pretty. If fortunate enough to stand in her presence without fear, you would notice her face. She appeared ageless, somewhat square faced, but it was those large jowls that come with age. She had a bad habit of snorting and sniffling when she spoke. No one was brave enough to comment on her eccentric behavior, for she was still very intimidating, and the animal next to her helped.

The woman stood next in line, and beside her was her large cat named My Pretty. It was not an ordinary feline. This oversized beast weighed over ten stones or close to 140 pounds. Its beautiful pelt was thick, gray, and luxurious. To add to the gray were black horizontal stripes that reflect a mixed parentage. When one would chance a view of this animal and look within the stunning striped face, it appeared hungry as it studied everything and everyone. In fact, someone had witnessed the animal as it was allowed to roam free and find its own food. As the cat prowled the castle floor within the length of its chain, a primal growl echoed within the great hall. As it was her turn to address the king, the animal was quieted.

"Beware the cat, ladies and gentlemen. She has not been fed, and unfortunately like her mistress, she becomes quite irritable when hungry." This said by the tall hooded woman as she cleared a large open swath and nodded to the throne. Many clung to the wall in hopes of not being noticed by this strange pairing. The cat appeared slow to respond, but her speed increased with the pull of the chain or a verbal command with a quick tug. Its quickness was demonstrated by its ability to cover surprising distances with short bounding leaps. The beast had now stopped to groom in a majestic reclining position, scanning all with its fierce golden eyes. Her mistress called out to her; the cat roared a deep-throated thunderous reply that echoed throughout the castle.

The king's guards were alerted yet formal, as they closed ranks around the king. Gustav stood to the front of the monarch. He was dressed in the militia's formal attire that included body armor that covered his upper torso. He held his shield at the ready. The monarch spoke to the lady. "Madam Barbarossa, please rest assured that all within our kingdom are being assessed a fair and equal tax. We need these funds to maintain our militia and our roads and provide for our people in times of need."

For a large woman, Barbarossa handled herself with grace and an almost omnipotent presence. The cloak she wore had padded shoulders, adding to her size, and within the cloak there were pockets of concealment for what may be deemed magical items of illusion. This day, the hood of her cloak was raised in such a way that only those to her direct front could see her face. Angus sat unflinchingly before her as he gazed into the eyes of this woman and saw her anger. He spoke again. "Madam, speak to me, and let the court know of your intentions."

Moments after the king's plea, the woman took a deep breath and exhaled. Looking toward the king, she slowly brought out a crooked stick from within the cloak. All within the guard closed ranks even more. She appeared to ignore all around and began to turn in a circle. With both hands, she held the wand to her breast and all watched as her steps became as a flowing graceful circle. The woman stopped at each of the four points of the compass and slowly pointed the stick at the king. Gustav spoke aloud through clenched teeth to his fellows. "Beware. Our king is at risk."

Then spoke the witch. Her voice was cold, penetrating, and clearly heard by all of those within the hall. Many were chilled with fear as her voice filled the great room. "An army, says you, my lord. What force do you need, when you have me? Focus point of emerald fire, run through his heart, my seething ire." As the words were spoken, the wand began to glow yellow, then from yellow to emerald green. Within a few breathless moments, a brilliant beam of jade light blazed toward throne. Its brief path led to the heart. It would be a quick death through witchcraft as the king flinched not and awaited. The witch knew not of Gustav; he was intense, quick, and loyal to the court.

The well-muscled young knight prided himself in physical activity. He sprang like a cat and held up his small round shield to deflect the deadly beam. The brilliant flash of light was deflected to the wall above the king as a loud gasp was heard from the court. The large cat screamed as only such a beast could when in distress. Chaos ensued, as all within the king's guard pounced on the wench, capturing her and her cat.

With a shower of small bits of stone, the king was saved. Gustav and several of the knights had tackled the woman. Others just as brave subdued the cat. Those that concentrated on the cat grabbed banners and blankets to hold the cat down without injury to the animal. Frightened, the beast howled and snarled for its mistress. Several of the guards who caught the cat received lacerations and cuts from the snarling beast. Barbarossa called out to the beautiful angry feline. Within moments of hearing her mistress's voice, it quieted. The wand had been recovered by the young hero and given to the master at arms. Gretchen carried the evil knurled limb away to be locked up in a secret place.

Though somewhat disheveled, the king called for silence and calm. He then walked up to the lady as she lay restrained on the floor. He spoke in a loud clear voice. "For this terrible threat to the kingdom, madam, you will be chained and taken to the dungeon deep within the castle with a twenty-four-hour guard. This will be done until an adequate punishment will be found for such treasonous action."

Ignoring the king, she kept looking around to each of the guards. She stopped moving and looked directly at Gustav. Though chained, she called to him in sticky sweetness, "Rest lightly, lad. You have embarrassed me. I will not be long." Just before she was gagged, she hollered out once more, "I will find you, lad."

High above the scene, among the rafters of the great hall sat a small pixie-like figure. She was a small but powerful "good witch" named Elizabeth. She spoke quietly to herself, "Dear sister, what have you done? I followed you in hopes of helping subdue your issues of revenge and anger. I'm sorry about the loss of your loved one. He was such a kind, sweet, powerful man. He lacked common sense, but he was very

CHAPTER SIX

CAPTURING THE WITCH

Barbarossa's love interest had felt above the law. He bragged that he could take on anyone at any time. He just picked the wrong person and lost. He was good with the sword, but the woman he fought was better. It was one of those ill-conceived duels to the death that happened with too much ale and so little thought. "Remember, my dear, he called out your name with his last breath." Elizabeth called out another telepathic greeting: "Sleep and rest, I'm here to help."

Barbarossa had been taken to a cell, deep under the castle. Chained, gagged, and blindfolded, she sat. She bit through the gag and hollered, *"Elizabeth?"* Those powerful words were heard by her sister. "Leave me alone." The guards also heard her cry out; they looked at each other and then looked throughout the dungeon for Elizabeth. They found no one in that dark place. One brave soul called out to Barbarossa, "Be still, witch, your Elizabeth is not here." Barbarossa turned toward the knight as he looked through the small barred window of her cell door. She stared him down; though she sat blindfolded, he felt her ire. He cautiously backed away from the door of her cell.

Elizabeth and the woman called Barbarossa were indeed sisters. They were also members of a coven, a small group of witches who sought protection from those who were hanging and executing anyone found to be a witch. Being the more powerful witch, Barbarossa had cast a spell on Elizabeth, shrinking her to a diminutive size. The smaller sister still had power to change her size, but for this difficult confrontation, she stayed small, like a pint-sized pixie. This was a form of protection for her sister, though Elizabeth was not very happy about her status. Barbarossa's real name was Catherine, and she had changed her name as a form of intimidation to all those who challenged her.

Many years before, Barbarossa was walking a country path one day when she found a small kitten. It was such a cute little cat, but it surprised her mistress as it began to grow and grow over a very short time until it was the large beast that was now her companion. To control her kitty, she had fashioned the large chain harness and leash. The cat was a hunter that usually found its own food. This beautiful animal with a gray pelt and black stripes added to the mystique of this very powerful sorceress.

Elizabeth followed her sister, though not out of love. It was her effort to try to change the outcome of spells her sister frequently cast in anger. Elizabeth knew sooner or later her sister's witching ways would prove difficult and dangerous. This evening, she knew that her sister was risking her life and the lives of others who may be considered witches. The tiny person in the rafters was tired as she conjured up a small pillow and rested. Barbarossa sat in the large chair enveloped in chains, blindfolded. Her eyes were closed as her thoughts turned to the cat. She called out to it in telepathy: "How is My Pretty?" The cat had been pacing around in a small cell several doors away from Barbarossa's. When it heard her mistress's voice, she roared and sprung at the door.

The door held, but the guard who was standing outside of the cell jumped back, shouting, "Good golly, that cat can roar!" This happened just as Gustav was starting his turn on watch. The young man smiled nervously at the guard and said nothing about his shout. He then whispered, "Reporting for duty, you may go. The witch and the cat are mine now." Barbarossa knew that Gustav was near. Sitting, enveloped in her large cloak and tightly wrapped in chains, she began to take slow deep breaths, expanding and contracting her girth. After this exercise, she was totally relaxed. She sat alone and listened, as this was the time for the changing of the guard. As she sat there totally relaxed, the ropes and chains slipped and loosened. She became one with the chair and began to search for a weakness. She called out quietly to the chair, "Hello, my lovely chair, may I investigate your nature? Oh my, you're so strong and stoutly built with pine pegs. *Oops*, I have found a weakness, and a peg that can be loosened.

I'll just reach around and surround it with my presence. I will now pull it out. There, I'm afraid that soon we will literally part company."

Slowly, the lady stood; she stretched, and she stretched again. She finally broke the chair. The chains, the ropes, and the chair collapsed at her feet, and the sorceress was free. Now freed from her bondage, she pulled off her blindfold and gag. None of the guards, including Gustav, noticed that she was free. They had moved her to a cell deep within the lower part of the castle. The cell was small, and the door was massive. It was designed for anyone they wished to totally isolate.

To get to both cells, one entered through a door that led down a circular stairway. This flight of stairs was wide enough for several soldiers to walk shoulder to shoulder. It could almost be described as an underground tower. There were just a few cells, and it was lit by oil lamps mounted on its ancient walls. The walkway was like a stone tunnel and was encased by a rock wall. No one knew why it was built; they only knew that it was a very quiet place to hold enemies of the realm. Sound carried very well in this strange dungeon, as a loud clear voice was heard. "I'm free." Barbarossa called out, as all within the castle knew that a battle would be forthcoming

As the king was escorting his wife to a waiting carriage, the queen, in all seriousness, looked at him and said: "My king, just behead her and be done with it. Protect the realm." The king nodded to his mate and sighed. "My dear," said he, "it is not so easy to dispense with such a witch. She has freed herself as we speak. My guards and I must find her and devise other ways to defang that wench. I must go now. Pray for us."

With a brief kiss, he sent the carriage to a neighboring castle for refuge. He then rushed to join his militia. Then the king and his small band of militia began a journey into the castle depths for a meeting with Barbarossa. The last man who entered closed the heavy dungeon door that opened to this lower level. The ancient hinges groaned an announcement of their entrance. The brass-banded door thundered a resounding challenge down through the depths of the steeply curving passage.

All the king's men became silent as they began the descent. Except for their heavy breathing and footfalls, there was a deathly silence. As they continued their descent, a chilling wailing sound cut through to their very souls as the cry of the sorceress resounded and called to them. This siren call caused a rain of mortared dust to come down as a bitter snow sprinkling upon them as they slowly descended. The armored party seemed to shrink in size the closer they came to the sorceress. Barbarossa was the one imprisoned, but the soldiers felt as one caged with a banshee. The air was thick and stifling; this humidity added tension to those of the court. Suddenly, as they had walked past the first of the cells, hurried footsteps echoed retreat of some of the fearful comrades. As they retreated, they called back, saying that they're going for reinforcements.

As all were descending, a door they had just passed shattered, and there was a howling rush of wind as they knew the hairy beast had escaped. They heard it descending; all turned and faced the wall in hopes that they would be spared. They felt the animals breath, heard the claws striking the ancient stones, as the cat rushed by them. It ignored those frail humans who clung to the wall.

Then they heard the woman. "Oh, My Pretty, were they mean to you? Now it is our turn." The king called a halt and then called down the wench, "Great sorceress, let us come up from the depths of this passage to end this conflict. Bring your furry companion and let us go up to the light and discuss your grievances." Then they heard loud laughter that appeared to mock them. With the tittering giggle, she called out, "You are the king and I am the witch, and now you wish to parlay in the light?" She laughed again as she spoke. "Some of your brave soldiers have deserted, brave king. Those poor souls who remain quiver at my power and may doubt your effectiveness.

"All right, to be fair I will count to ten before I send my cat scampering up after stragglers. My precious will be quick, as she is with all game." In the fading light of the candles, they all looked around for reassurance. Gustav called out, "Wench, it is me you desire. Let the others depart, and I will continue to enter your domain. Let me meet your precious, and I will defang the beast. Let us meet in battle, and I will silence you." Gustav then looked at the king and his companions and then asked them all to leave. He took a deep breath and checked his sword; alone, he continued the spiraling descent.

The passageway seemed endless; as he came around one of the curving walls, he met the witch. She appeared startled and then smiled at him wickedly: "Bright young lad, you surprised me. Now what shall we do? Battle?" She laughed again and held out her arms in a supplicant gesture of greeting. "You stand at the threshold of doom. The beast awaits you in the darkness. We stand in a never-ending pit. There is no way out, except through me and my terrible power." Suddenly Gustav lunged at her with his sword. His saber cut through an illusion of the lady and sparked against the stone wall.

He then heard her scream derisively. The voice called, "My Pretty, find him, eat him. Now!" He heard the roar, as the beast charged. In great leaps of feline grace, the beast raced up the stairs, reaching another illusion. In playful ignorance, the cat stepped gingerly through the likeness. Sitting before this magical picture, the cat tried pawing it. Then she lay flat and rolled over on her back, not knowing what to do next. Looking around somewhat puzzled, she heard her mistress's voice: "Finished? I suggest that you find the lad before I turn you into a dirty old rock."

CHAPTER SEVEN

GOOD VERSUS EVIL

The cat had not far to go to find the knight. Gustav heard the cat, and he prepared for the attack. The cat heard him on the stairs, saw him, and leaped. The cat and Gustav noticed that everything was slowing down as in a dream. All stopped, and they heard a tiny elfin voice say, "Kings X, my dears." Even Barbarossa was frozen in place as she had followed the cat; everything was frozen except her mouth. "Well, well. If it isn't my little sister and her Kings X spells. Too little, too late, my dear, my ca-ca-cat wwillllllll—"

She was frozen midsentence in a comical pause. In a twinkling flash of light, a petite, gray-haired matron appeared. "Oh, such a twiddle, so little time, and I must be quick." With those words, she magically picked up Gustav and moved him up the stairs, and opening dungeon door, she placed him standing against the wall. With Gustav on the outside, the door to the pit closed solidly, and she returned to face her sister. Elizabeth moved to within a few feet of her sister and the cat; she had a frown on her face and hands on her dainty hips. She said, "Sister of mine, you really are quite a pain in my backside. This anger of yours is going to cause you to end up in a puff of green smoke. Now to keep you and your beast quiet for a moment, I will chant. See you later." She then began a chant:

"I see spiral stairs with endless swirl.
They are not mine, but I'll give a whirl.
Close this pit, lock it up.
Please, keep the witch with the snarling pup.

Please move it on a little mile.
Let this kingdom rest a while.
After that, let brave souls meet.
To battle the witch, her wrath, and the four clawed feet."

The ground shook and rumbled as the strange underground tower disengaged itself from the fortress. The dungeon door disappeared as the underground tower was now as a magical mole. It moved through the ground. Great rocks moved and soil displaced until it stopped about a mile away. It was like a giant moving scar above the ground as great rifts were made then filled. All above ground were frightened by this tumultuous sight within and without the fortress. It appeared as an earthquake that many of the Valley had never seen or even heard of before. "That will have to do. Good luck to you all." This said by the tiny good witch.

Somewhere in time, a clock struck twelve. Then deep within the bowels of the earth, the cat, held in surprise, suddenly realized that it would now land on her mistress's head. It was a glancing blow to the illusion of her mistress as the feline sailed past and hit the wall with all four paws. It quickly slid down the ancient stone wall and landed on the floor. It then rolled into a ball, waiting for kickoff. Carefully, the beast looked up to the smiling illusion and began to run up the stairs. It was an endless spiral. As the old saying goes, "What goes around comes around." In a quick, surprisingly short ascent, the cat came again behind her mistress. Confused and not knowing if this was another illusion, it sat grooming itself for a few moments. She gave a small, weak domesticated meow. There was no response as the witch, puzzled, was trying to regain her bearings. This time, the cat let out a very long and loud scream. This approach worked, as her mistress jumped and quickly turned to face her cat, saying, "Bad, wicked, kitty."

The large animal laid its head down at the feet of the powerful woman, seeking, as it appeared, forgiveness. "My pretty, pretty beast, such a look of repentance. Let us find a way out of here. You must find the key stone. I know that my sister would leave this key to the puzzle. It's just a little stone that when we push it in and say I'm sorry, the spell is forgotten and we may leave. Then they will feel my wrath." The animal knew what to do and began sniffing the wall looking for the key. The oil lamps began to burn brighter with a spell from the sorceress.

Many groans and growls were heard coming from the cat. The witch called out to her sister, "You're not very nice. I will make it worth your while, if you remove this spell. Nevertheless, I think my cat has found the answer. See you soon, my dear." All heard the low rumble of moving earth as the underground tower slowly returned and engaged the dungeon. Once more, the door appeared that led down the circular passageway. To one side of the door stood Gustav and the king, with others who had rejoined the quest. "Are you sure you want to meet this sorceress alone?" "Sire, I'm the one who twisted the cat's tail, and I must be the one to remove its fangs." "I wish not to lose you, my boy. Just be careful and return to us."

The king and all who were with him wished Gustav success. A strange, chill breeze came through the passageway as he opened the door. "We will watch your sweetheart and keep her from harm," called one of the men. "I'll not be gone that long," Gustav called as he began to enter. Suddenly, all heard the roar of the cat and lilting voice of Barbarossa as she called, "He's here, My Pretty. We're ready for you, my lad." The door behind him slammed shut as he entered, and with a brilliant flash, it appeared to be welded shut. The light from the passageway still flickered beneath the door. The captain of the guard called for an ax. "We're coming for you, boy." An ax was found, and the strongest among them made the first strike. It struck the door, and there it stayed, as no one could remove it.

The king stood near the door, quieting the excited troops; he placed his hand on the door. All the others crowded next to him, and each one placed their hand on the door. "We'll be here for you, Gustav." They all shouted in affirmation, and they began a quiet vigil. He heard those behind the door; he too reached back and touched the door. He then turned and began the descent to meet the woman and the cat. Resting his hand on the hilt of his sword, he looked around him and felt a presence. It was not the sorceress or the cat, it was something else. He felt the warming glow, and startled, he called out, "Who is here? Be wary, for we are both in danger. Speak up so that I may know with whom I die."

CHAPTER EIGHT

GODMOTHER'S MAGIC

Though usually very small, Elizabeth decided to make herself known to the young man. She transformed herself into a slightly larger shape and being. As he saw her standing in the air, he was speechless. But he had the presence of mind to ask, "Who are you, tiny one?"

"Young man, you may call me Elizabeth. I have become your godmother, and you may consider me a giver of small acts of kindness and magic." "Can you protect me, Elizabeth?" "My spells are tiny compared to my oversized sister. There are times when I can counter or diminish her spells and sometimes not. This is not to say I can change things back—I just try to help them become more positive. Please, William Gustav, I have no idea what she's up to, but I'll be here."

As Gustav began the descent once more, there was a blinding light that appeared to penetrate every nook and cranny. He stopped, closed his eyes, and waited for the challenge. He had entered with only his sword, and as the light diminished, he looked up on the wall and saw an old shield hanging slightly above him. It was a tarnished relic of wars past. He carefully removed great shield and held it close to his body. He heard the roar of the cat and felt the evil presence of the sorceress.

He looked up the stairway and called out, "You have my heart, Ariel. I will return to touch your sweet lips." Barbarossa spoke to her partner. "How sad, My Pretty. This dear boy wishes to return to his sweetness." Taking a slow, deep breath, he prepared for battle. He stepped back and stayed close to the wall. His breastplate glowed with a brightness and newness of his position. The shield was in stark contrast. It was tarnished from years on the wall; it was old and bore marks of an unknown battle. His sword was slowly withdrawn from its scabbard and brought to the ready. Not accustomed to this shield, he still felt comfort in holding the relic.

As the light returned to the faint flickering light of the oil lamps, he smelled the cat, and then he saw it approaching. "My Pretty, I presume." The animal roared and the incredible sound reverberated throughout the staircase. "I think my furred beast is upset with you, William. She's hungry and not very particular at what or who she eats.

I'm more upset than she. Thus, it is I who shall punish you." With those spoken words, she brought out a second wand that she had hidden in her cloak. It too began to glow yellow and then quickly produced a green blazing light that flashed toward the young knight. Again, the streak of piercing light was deflected as it hit the old relic he was holding. It was directed to the ceiling, where heavy blocks of stone began to rain down upon Gustav and the sorceress. These stones were the lining of the tunnel walls. The builders of the dungeon had fortunately built it to last. This inner wall was what was collapsing upon Gustav and the witch. He held the shield above his head as the inner layer fell. The weight was great, as he was knocked down. He huddled as best he could under the shield. Unfortunately, his legs still stuck out and received many punishing blows from the rockfall. He groaned and tried to pull his legs up under the shield. Elizabeth called to him as he cried out in pain. "Keep crawling under the shield, my boy." He heard her voice. "Think small, and make it fit," she cried.

Gustav thought small as he closed his eyes and kept imagining that he was pulling in his arms and his legs. Then he realized that the spell had worked. He felt and heard the heavy stones rain down upon the shield, and none were hitting him. The shield felt immense as he appeared to shrink. "Thank you, godmother." "Thank me not, my boy, until the spell of reverse. Quietly, feel your hands and your feet. My sister is still alive, and she still wishes you harm." Gustav carefully felt what should have been his hands and his feet. He was shocked, as now claws of a beast were his. He quickly covered his mouth and screamed. "Please, be silent, my gentle boy. She will hear you. You must believe me and know that this spell can be reversed. You must leave here and find a place to grow in peace. Do you hear me?" In rasping gasps, he answered, "Yes, godmother, please be quick."

My Pretty, not a beast to dawdle, swiftly ran looking for her mistress as the heavy stone blocks rained all around. One even glanced off her muscled body. Still, she ran toward the voice of her mistress as she called for help. The cat stopped momentarily and found shelter in a small alcove. The falling stones appeared to stop, and the dust of the ancient mortar billowed like gray smoke; the cat groomed and listened.

Barbarossa felt the first of the ceiling stones as they fell, striking her on the head. "I'm a strong and powerful witch. These will not harm me." More of the ancient stone fell, finally knocking her down, covering the witch. "Save me, My Pretty, take my hand and pull me from this rubble." Silence answered her call, and she listened for others within this tomb. "I will find you, young knight. You will not be spared. Call out, and I will make it quick but not painless."

The sorceress heard the news of the spell Elizabeth had given Gustav, and she giggled. She winced at her pain, but she thought to herself: "A spell of permanence, how delightfully wicked." She continued to think, and then she said: "Something to remember me by." She reached through the rocks wherein she was covered, carefully pushing the wand through the stones. Though her voice was weak and growing faint, she chanted, "No Kings X to save this boy, hold the spell, he's just a toy. He'll squeak and plead in years to come. He's much larger than my thumb. He'll search for miles to find a place, I wish I were there to see his face. His face of shock to see his love, she's coming fast, quick as a dove. The woman now has met her sweet. Though instead of a kiss, she plans to eat. This poor knight, so brave and true, will now be gone, oh boo-hoo." *I know it's not much of a chant, but what does one expect under all these rocks.* She coughed and laughed as the spell was cast. Gustav would feel something happen, but he had other things on his mind at that moment.

Her voice was fading; she had dropped the wand and found the strength to reach around to her only friend. "Oh, My Pretty, I will miss you. Now go and make me proud." Gustav had crawled out from under the shield; he stood and found a strange giant world. The stones gave the landscape a feel of total desolation. He then heard the piercing screech. He called to Elizabeth, "Godmother, the time is far spent. I have little remaining until the beast finds me." The good witch lightly scolded him, saying, Gustav, I didn't go to all this trouble just to have you eaten by that oversized cat. Head up the stairs, and get a move on." As he began scampering up over and around the many stones, he learned quickly how to maneuver his body. Down below the spiral steps, the large woman coughed again and whispered to her pretty cat, "You cannot save me." The large feline called softly and pawed the hard stones that encased her mistress.

"Listen and be still, My Pretty. Gustav is out there in the rubble, and he is much smaller. He's just a little furry snack, but he will be so much fun to catch." She giggled once more and coughed in pain. "Goodbye, my good little kitty." Curling wisps of green smoke signaled the mortal end of this witch. Elizabeth felt a sharp pain in her heart, and she knew that her sister had passed. Crying softly, she said, "Though you were a handful, my dear, I will miss our memories as Sisters of Life. I will make sure your kitty is not harmed. I love you, Catherine, dear sister."

The hunt had begun by the cat. The spiral pit was full of dark shadows, as many of the oil lamps had been knocked off the wall when the great stones fell. Gustav realized that his sight was quite good in the dim light. The knight was moving as fast as possible in his sleek white ferret body. The spell that Elizabeth had given him included coloring that appeared as his clothing. He was a sleek white ferret with dark markings. He was wearing one article of clothing. It was a belt that held a tiny sword. "It's such a long ways up to the door." Then he heard the scrambling, running sound of a four-legged beast. "The cat is alive." Up and over and under the boulders, he moved like a ferret. He heard a faint voice calling to him. It was the wheezing sound of the witch's last words.

"I'm sorry, dear boy. I can't be there to see you and my cat when you dance the last waltz. There will be one more surprise. If you and the cat don't get along, then"—she paused—"I'll never tell. You'll love the irony in this . . . surprise! Her strange giggling faded into dark silence.

He tried to arrange his tiny sword, as it seemed so small, even for him. He then continued running. His strength increased as he even controlled his tail. Briefly stopping, he pulled out the tiny pin and held it in his claws. He thought to himself and laughed, "Oh, if I could be seen by the king and my friends. I think we would all have a great laugh." Gustav stood for a moment, listening for his pursuer. He shook off the fear and had a good laugh. If simple beings as the ferret could laugh or cry, Gustav was doing both as a continued up the stairs, seeking the top. He listened for the angry furry beast that pursued him.

Prowling up the stairs, she had heard her prey. She crouched and, with stealth, crept up the stairs. She missed her only friend in this unforgiving world. Her motivation was find it, catch it, and snack on it. The cat met the small ferret knight and simply crouched down to look into the eyes of her snack. Feeling for a gallant moment, he reached for his sword and pulled it out with gusto. Unfortunately, he couldn't hold it very well with his ferret claws, and the pin slipped from his grasp. The tiny sword flew toward the beast, where it stuck rather soundly onto My Pretty's nose.

The cat looked rather comical as it tried to shake off the diminutive weapon that was stuck on her muzzle. It came loose quickly, and now the large gray cat looked rather angry as it eyed young Gustav. On the final step, the cat began to circle her prey. Her beautiful tail was waving like a snake preparing to strike. Then it stood with its back to the door, blocking his way out. The cat's appendage stopped the snake-like movement as the cat prepared to strike.

Gustav's tiny heart beat a staccato pulse; his breath was wheezing from the dusts and tremendous effort it took to climb the monstrous steps. Trying not to laugh or cry, he faced the cat as she roared and roared again in remembrance of her mistress's last command. As her body tensed, her muscles rippled with anticipation as she prepared to pounce. Like a coiled spring, she leaped toward her prey. Again, it was noticed by the cat that her movements were slowing until she was stopped in midair. The cat screeched, but she just hung in the air. Staring at the cat suspended above, he called, "Elizabeth, how much time do I have?"

"Good question, Gustav. Let's see," she said as she scratched her dimpled chin, calculating. "Time versus spell versus . . . *whoops.* You must run now . . ." He ran with all his might as he squeezed quickly beneath the cat and under the door. Just as he crawled beneath the massive door, he heard the great cat roar. "Thanks, godmother!" Though frozen in space, the cat watched as the white ferret crawled under her.

Unfrozen, She turned in one fluid motion and leaped to where her prey should be. The landing was smooth, knowing the ferret was under one of the paws; she carefully lifted each paw, one after another. She found nothing there. And from deep within her body, she let out a mournful howl. As Gustav took a deep breath, he looked back under the door. Beneath the door he saw a strange and comical sight. It was a cat's eye staring at him from an odd angle. As she clawed at the door in a futile effort to come through, she saw the ferret. He was so close and yet unreachable. As the gentleman he was, even as a ferret, he saluted the beast with a tiny bow.

It was like pouring salt on a wound or twisting the tiger's tail; the reception from the cat was far from gracious. He felt the wind of her breath as he heard the ferocious roar. Trying not to mock the cat, he casually waved goodbye to the imprisoned furry beast. He quickly moved away from those who were trying to break through the door. A few of them, including Gretchen, were puzzled as they saw the white ferret squeeze under the door and quickly crawl to a perch above them.

The sleek little beast appeared to be watching them. "What an odd little animal, was that someone's pet?" said the king. With that question unanswered, they all returned to the business at hand, that of cutting down the door and rescuing Gustav. "Godmother, is there a way I may communicate with my love or my friends?" "Dear, you have been speaking to me through your thoughts." "I think, I speak, and I communicate. Oh, thank you, Elizabeth." "You have much to do in your coming life, said his tiny protector." "How do I speak to others?" "The same way you speak to me. Just look at who you're silently speaking to. Then you must be persistent until they hear you. Talk to them as you would face-to-face." He looked at the king and those who were helping break down the door. He heard many comments as they touched his soul.

"I should've been there with him!" Gretchen shouted. The others quickly countered her comment. Angus, a fellow knight, and the king placed their arms around her. He then said to all, "We will find him." The monarch walked away from the group to gather his thoughts. He hadn't walked far when he suddenly heard a familiar voice. "Your Highness, are you free?

"What, who, where are you, Gustav?" The king had a dazed and bewildered look on his face as others looked at him. He seemed slightly confused as he walked through the main hall. He began to absentmindedly whistle. "Where are you, my boy? Please show yourself." The middle-aged, silver-haired leader appeared to nonchalantly look behind curtains, under chairs, and generally appeared to be acting very odd to those around. He also appeared to be talking to himself. "Sire, please stop and rest on that bench." The man sat and continued looking around, crossing and uncrossing his legs and taking slow deep gulps of air.

"You are my King?" said the young knight. "Yes, I am," responded the king as he looked around for the source of the voice. The young knight's voice was heard again: "I am with you. I just cannot be seen. I have been spelled. In fact, I'm a beast." The look on the king's face dissolved into one of sadness. As he sat, he bent down, rubbing his face, as one washing. He held his chin with praying hands, closed his eyes, and asked, "You are a beast?" "Not the fire-breathing, village-destroying myth, sir, just one that can't meet with friends face-to-face."

"May I see you?" "No Sire, It is better to mourn and remember me as I once was. I will be with you occasionally. Please, how is Ariel?" "She was crushed with grief. When she heard the news, she ran up to me with smiling expectations. She looked at my face, stopped, and immediately knew. She collapsed in grief. I had her carried over to a small alcove for privacy. I am going over there now to make sure that she is okay." As Gustav watched, the king walked over to the beautiful young woman who was his betrothed. She had quieted and glanced up to the king; she tearfully stated, "If there was just a chance that my love could whisper once more sweet thing to me, I would desire this, my lord." He tried to console her. Her face was pale; her cheeks were red from tears of loss.

She still was radiant, as one could see that sweet upturned smile. It penetrated the heart of her silent, invisible love. Finally, he could stand it no longer and whispered her name. "Ariel?" She looked around with a pleading yet fearful look. She called to him, "What, who? My love, is that your voice I hear?" "Ariel, I had your heart at the tip of my sword, and now you have mine at the tip of your tongue." The king spoke to the two young lovers with grieving tears. As he spoke, one could see tears flowing down his tanned and creased cheeks. He cleared his throat and spoke. "I will leave you now." He then turned to Ariel. "You have our love, our thoughts, and prayers. Be well, blessed be your love, and enjoy whatever time you have in life." Closing his eyes, he thought of poem that came to his mind:

"No lips to tease, no eyes one sees or soft breast to lay my head.
Just words my love of feelings strong, to each heart today is led.

Above the mortal's earthly plain,
You, my children fly.
Now enjoy the sun, the moon, and sparkling stars across the wondrous
Sky."

Saying no more, he turned away quietly and left Ariel and the "voice" of Gustav alone. Looking around anxiously, Ariel spoke. "Please talk and tell me of this experience. Let me know of this evil that has robbed me of your warmth." He had an idea, then spoke. "With great reluctance, I ask you to hold out your hand and do not scream or move abruptly." The voice of Elizabeth chimed in. "Please, William Gustav, I'm not sure of this action or its consequence."

"Who was that?" asked the young woman. "My godmother. She's watching over us, and she worries a lot. Please close your eyes and hold out your hand. I will be there in a moment." said the ferret. Ariel held out her hand and closed her eyes. She thought of the king's message of hope and cheer. She felt movement of a creature on her hand. She heard him say, "Listen to my voice and then open your eyes, look to your hand, and remember that it is a spell."

There was a sudden intake of breath signaled that she had seen the creature in her hand. A scream registered her shock and disbelief in the terrible calamity which befell her sweetness and once–future mate. Looking at the ferret, she felt a strangeness overtake her. Her thoughts grew hazy, and she felt as though she was changing. She called to Elizabeth, "Help me, godmother. The strangeness I feel, it is as though I'm becoming something else and I'm looking at the ferret and I am feeling very, very hungry." "Barbarossa, you are an evil sorceress!" Elizabeth called her sister's name in vain, for now she knew of the surprise her sister had promised. "Gustav, you must run for your life and run from your love." As he began to run, he heard Elizabeth, "I am sorry. My sister has left you a final trap. She was very good with evil magic. Run for your life and for Ariel's as well.

CHAPTER NINE

FLYING LESSONS

"Why, she'll get over it. It may take a while, but we are in love." "Please run to the ledge at the top of the wall, and you will see." The small ferret knight ran quickly up the wall and to a ledge. He turned and looked down upon the scene. "Oh, my Ariel, what have I done?" he cried as he saw her. "She is now your mortal enemy. My sister has left a bitter surprise for your sweet, caring love. Your Ariel now wishes to have you for dinner. I am not sure that a protecting spell will save you. If she were to attack and devour you, her heart will be filled with remorse, and she too would die."

As Elizabeth finished speaking, the great raptor rose on wings of flight and sought the high ceilings. All in the castle were startled by the scream of the eagle. A rain of tiny feathers came down as the few little brown birds that roosted in the rafters scattered in noisy chaos and sought refuge throughout the castle. This allowed room for the great flying hunter as she found a perch. It was a very tight fit for the immense bird with keen vision.

As this feathered creature looked about, she saw the ferret on the ledge. Quickly launching, the female dove with rocketing speed, raking her talons against the stone wall and barely missing Gustav as he found shelter behind a stone gargoyle. "Gustav, please call to the king."

"We can't harm her, godmother." "No, my dear, we must call for help to escort her through the great hall and out the door to freedom." "She will be lost to the winds." "Please trust me, my boy. You are her first prey, and she will not leave the vicinity until she finds and consumes you. She was as a human and she continues as an eagle: very determined." Gustav searched for the king, and he was found talking to several of his assistants as he observed the huge bird in flight. As a group, they were pondering the strange events that they had witnessed. Some whispered, "Black magic," and others referred to this as part of the huge full moon. Seeing their king responding and directing his people so positively reassured them that all would be well . . .

"My king, we must speak," said the young knight. "Where have you been Gustav?" "Sire, if we are to talk, let us find a quiet place that is secluded and away from the curious folk of the kingdom." "I know of a secluded alcove above the great hall. There we can observe the great bird." Occasionally, all watched as the golden eagle would glide briefly above the hall and then dive to just above the floor in search of its prey. She was appearing very agitated in the confines of the immense hall; many within the hall were also seeking shelter. The great bird had a look of fierceness and majesty as she sought the ferret.

"What does this bird of prey have to do with the spell that is upon you?" "Sire, that bird in flight is my Ariel. With an anguished voice that resonated throughout the hall, he cried, "Oh gracious, that is your love, spelled?" "This is why she must be released to fly free, my king. In time, this spell may be countered, but now she needs flight and freedom. She is a wild and natural creature." "Fly, she will. We will help her to the door." This said by the monarch as he called for help.

To the consternation of the gossips in the castle, the king spoke no more to anyone about the bird or spells or witches. Instead, he continued to order all available help to assist in moving or herding the bird through the great hall and out the massive doors. "Let us be careful, people, the bird only seeks her freedom." The captain of the guard looked at his father and then to the large raptor. He quietly held open his arms in a questioning glance and mouthed the words, "What happened here?" The king called, "Later, my son." The captain had organized all to move quietly and carefully in order to funnel the bird toward the great doors. The great doors were slowly opened, and all moved away from the entrance so as not to distract. Those in the great hall who were helping moved through the castle, speaking quietly. Some slowly waved the large pennants which hung from the walls. Others found quiet places to sit and observe the beautiful eagle in flight. Though mysterious as it appeared, many were mesmerized by the sight of this beauty of nature and magic.

Finally, the great eagle appeared to see the open door and glided gracefully on large, silent wings into the evening. Many felt a rush of air as the bird flew low over their heads. "I will find you, Ariel. We will be reunited." Gustav silently called. When reaching the free air, the great one screeched a greeting to the night. The novice aviator soared and was silhouetted against the dying embers and changing hues of her first sunset. Pangs of hunger called, and the great one sought prey. In the country, she feasted but never forgot the ferret.

She would hunt until she found him in the coming hours or days. "Thank you for your help, sire. She'll be happier for now in flight." The king spoke quietly with emotion as he said, "As she flew through the doorway, my heart ached as a father saying farewell to a child. Find her, my boy." Gustav voiced a farewell to the king and then found a quiet niche for protection and solace. He also sought Elizabeth. "Godmother, what should I do to reunite with Ariel?" "You must rest, Gustav. We will seek her in the daylight, when she might be resting. Please, sleep till the morning hours, and then tomorrow, you must then tread lightly."

Through the night, sleep was a fitful adventure for all within the castle walls who pondered what may have transpired. The great golden raptor, though immature, was like a young novice learning flight. She flew high above the castle, searching for the small ferret. Tiring of the search, she sought small game in the open fields to satisfy her hunger pangs. She found a perch on the limb of the great tree that overlooked the Valley. Normally, she would hunt during daylight hours: but tonight she enjoyed her first flight. The full moon drew the bird up to enjoy the cool night air. Some folks had seen her beautifully silhouetted against the rising sphere of the night.

There was sparkling dew upon the grass as the sun rose. Some creatures began their sleep cycles, and others greeted the day. The long night had tired the great raptor. She looked over the valley and observed people, dogs, cats, and even rats. She immediately sought flight as she saw the ferret leaving the castle and entering her domain. In human form, he knew the castle well: as a small ferret, he was intimidated by the size of his surroundings.

Gustav had crawled along ledges and windowsills of the castle and found a small opening. He watched from the small opening in the fortress wall as the common people began to enter through the gate. Some folks had just learned of the strange incident. Many looked to the sky in hopes of seeing the large bird. Soldiers leaving on patrol and above on the wall chose not to speak of the happening. They tried to return the castle to a normal day. Gretchen could be seen standing near the castle doors. Watching her, she appeared detached and lost in thought. He carefully walked along ledges and narrow spaces until he was above her. He then projected a greeting to her. "Gretchen?" With a hopeful expression, she whirled around, looking for the source of the voice. "Show yourself, knight, and report." A small voice called to her. "Please find a private place, and we will talk." Looking around and trying to find the source of the voice, she walked away from the great door and found a tree. She leaned against the tree and spoke to her old friend. "Gustav, why have you taken so long to reach me?" He spoke of both spells and their tragic consequences. She brought a gloved hand to her mouth to stifle a cry of anguish.

"Oh, my dear friend, I had but a glimpse of your love. I am so crushed that the witch ended such a blossoming love." "All is not lost. I can still speak to people, and I'm going to find my love and change the spell." "You've always been a little bit crazy. How in the world do you plan this? I can just see you standing there with their arms outstretched and calling her name." "Not a bad idea. I must be going. We will talk again."

She looked around and called again to the voice. "Wait, Gustav!" "What is it, friend?" "Please don't be offended, but may I keep your shield until you return?" "Only if you promise to clean it." The ferret laughed a squeaky little giggle. "Certainly," he said. She raised the shield that she held and embraced it. She then rested her chin on the top of the old relic, and with tears coursing down her cheeks, she said her farewell. "I will keep it polished and ready for your return."

After that brief tearful farewell, he quickly ran away from his hidden perch. He found his way down the great wall and ran into some bushes for cover and concealment. Gustav then climbed one of the tall bushes to get his bearings and possibly catch a glimpse of his nemesis and love. Slowly and cautiously, he glanced up for any signs of attack.

He heard the screech and a rushing wind as the great eagle sought her prey. The sharp talons raked the top of the bush, barely missing the top of his head. Gustav ducked quickly. Gustav's heart was rebounding with a staccato pulse of fear as he dove for cover. He saw the large eyes of golden fierceness as their eyes met, and suddenly, he felt very, very cold. "William, find a rabbit hole," said the elfin voice. He saw one about ten ferret lengths away. He hesitated, for it seemed such a very far ways to go. "You must run quickly, for she will find you soon."

The young ferret knight glanced at the rabbit hole, saying, "Do you think it's occupied?" With an exasperated sigh, she said, "William Gustav, I don't think that occupancy is a problem as much as your speed to the hole." "Elizabeth, I believe I have another solution. You may not like it, but it will give all the time I need." "Please tell me, young ferret." "There is a large log over there with a small tunnel under it. If I were to stand and entice my feathered damsel to try for me again and she were to miss, I would have more time to reach the entrance to the rabbit's den."

"You, spellbound ferret, are daft! Your eagle-sized love may just stop and wait for you to come out, don't you think?" She sighed and said not a word as Gustav ran for the log. He crawled into the hole just as the eagle raked the top of the log with her sharp talons. He then crawled out from under the log and climbed to the top. He was almost nonchalant as he stood there, looking up to the eagle as she prepared to dive again. He then raised his arms in a gesture of greeting. "Just how long do you plan on waiting, William?" asked his elfin godmother. She watched and held her breath and counted to three. As the great bird zeroed in on the little one, she feared for the ferret's life and decided to help him along.

The good witch pointed her petite wand at him and gave it in upward twitch and watched. Within seconds, Gustav was lifted up, magically facing the great talons. "Please give a big welcome to your sweet love." He had little time as he impacted her leg. Immediately, he held on for his dear life. In a more subdued and muffled call, he asked, "What do I do now, Elizabeth?" "There is a golden rope in your claws that needs to be tied and knotted around your love's leg." The ferret found himself buffeted by the winds of flight. Finally, after holding with great difficulty, he was able to firmly grasp the tiny gold rope. He held onto it as though his life depended on it, for it did. "Wait until she returns to her perch, then you will quickly wrap it around her leg and tie it into a knot."

With an immense rushing of wing, the great bird landed. She began looking for the small creature that had attacked her leg. Gustav was holding as best he could and then was holding on with one claw. He began swinging the rope around the leg. "It is not working, Elizabeth," he said as he dodged the large raptor, as she kept trying to catch the rope.

"Listen to me: Whip it back and forth, and as you do this, let out more rope until you see the other end. Do it quickly, or she will win your game." Indeed, the bird continued trying to grab at the tiny rope but fortunately kept missing. Gustav started calling to the bird in his little squeaky ferret's voice and, at the same time, began whipping the rope around the leg. Soon, he saw the other end and grabbed it with his other claw, almost falling off in the process. As he now he hung to both ends of the rope, he called out, "Success, Elizabeth! Now what do I do?"

"A simple over and under knot will do." Remembering some prior life instruction, he pulled the rope over and then under as he stood shaking on the great claw. As the knot was secured, the great raptor quieted and appeared to be frozen in position. Gustav whispered to his good witch, "Now, what do I do?" "Call to her, Gustav." "Ariel, my love, speak."

The large raptor bent down as far as it could and cast an eye at the creature that was now holding on to her leg. With a curious blink, she began to think/speak: "How curious our circumstance, dear ferret—I your mortal enemy, no longer hunger for you as a small snack. Instead, I feel sadness for what we have lost."

He could hear Elizabeth give a sigh as he relaxed and just stood there, looking up to the beautiful eyes of his transformed love. He then cautiously climbed onto the immense talons and thought, "I cannot say that I don't quake at your presence, but I am grateful to hear your thoughts. My beating heart is relieved to hear those thoughts as they penetrate my soul." They spoke quietly of the events of the past week. "I really didn't want to interrupt until you both had time to catch up. You have questions that are valid, and there are several answers. Are you ready for the answers?" "Before we find the answers, I wish to take my young love for a view of all that surrounds us." "Please do," said Elizabeth. "It will help clear your minds and possibly refocus you on your lives."

Gustav held tightly to the rope as a large bird sought flight. As her wings moved in graceful arcs, the two climbed high above the Valley. She finally found thermals of air that provided lift as she and the ferret soared in high flight.

"How do you like soaring?" she asked. "Can I open my eyes?" "Please do." "Oh my goodness. So this is what you see of the universe?" As his claws clung tightly to the rope, his body was lifted by the rushing air. "Hold on, brave knight, the magic of flight will cleanse your soul as we become one with the sky." They took a soaring dive as if to impact the earth. Then she pulled up in level flight.

"See the fortress of our king, the farms, and our beautiful home. Look at the tiny ants, actually people of our land who go about their labors. My young knight, I believe this will begin our travels. That is, when our Mistress Elizabeth tells us of our choices. What say you tiny, elfin witch?" "Oh, my children, there is much to do, if you wish. First choice is to stay in this wonderful valley and fly the thermals and observe the kingdom. The second choice is by your own Magic—answer calls for help wherever they are located."

They called in unison, "When do we leave, great witch?" This was the first time since it all started that they felt their love as it had first begun. In the early evening, Ariel had taken flight, leaving Gustav to hunt for his dinner. By nightfall, they had both returned to a large tree that stood above the valley. He had found a tunnel beneath her stand as she rested on a large branch high above.

CHAPTER TEN

CALL TO MAGIC

The rising sun had awakened them both, and again they separated briefly to find nourishment. They finally called a greeting to each other. "Good morning." Gustav remarked, "Our first morning, dear one." "It was not as I imagined," she said with a sigh. Elizabeth interrupted, "I think it is time to practice a pickup procedure." "I don't think I can pick her up," said Gustav. "Don't be silly, ferret," said the good witch. "It is one thing to catch a fish in water and eat it, but it is quite another to grab a ferret who faces you with arms outstretched."

Ariel was now in flight overhead when Gustav called to her, "Can you see me, my sweet?" The eagle was confused as she veered upward and then swooped toward the earth. "You certainly caught my attention from such a great distance, my ferret. I've noticed that indeed you are a white ferret, but I've also noticed the strange coloring to parts of your body." "It would be difficult to give him clothes, so I just colored him an overcoat," said the good witch. "Now that I focus on it, it does look like a little dark jacket. Where is your sword?"

Laughingly, Gustav answered. "Oh, I left that with the cat." As they were conversing, no one appeared to notice danger approaching from a distance. The large striped panther remembered the ferret. My Pretty had matured quickly and, now separated from the influence of her mistress, was a hunter in the Valley. Her first prey was in sight, and she was not going to miss this time.

Gustav found a large boulder on which to stand. The eagle circled and then saw Gustav. "Gustav, look at me and open your arms, quickly," she said with urgency to her voice." I will pick you up between my talons. Relax, my love, I done this many times before, and I rarely miss when I fish. Only this time I am not going to eat you. I'll just embrace you and lift you up to new heights. Here I come."

The eagle saw danger and said nothing; she gently folded back her wings to increase her speed. As she approached, the cat was preparing to pounce. "Close your eyes and greet me." In a quick moment, the great eagle embraced her love just as the great cat sprung with a well-muscled spring. The cat roared in frustration as Gustav was lifted up out of harm's way into the sky by his sweet feathered love. As the cat Landed on all four paws, it was as if that part of her life had finished. Gustav was no longer on her mind; she now only wished to hunt, find a mate, and live as she should in the wild.

Gustav clung to the leg of his feathered love, and he looked down on where he had just been. He saw the castle, the valley, and he also realized that the cat had barely missed him. He looked up at the golden raptor which carried him high in the sky. Then he called to her, "You saved my life. I thank you."

"You are very worth that effort. I think My Pretty will do just fine. She appeared to be headed toward the mountains. If she's lucky, she will find a mate and live a good natural life. That life will be without magic or spells or witchcraft, and it will be good." "I hope you two have noticed that the rope around your leg is no longer needed. Now you may notice that there is a better way to attach yourself to your love's leg." Gustav looked at the line that he had been holding on to and realized that was actually a small seat. As the winds pulled at him, he was able to maneuver himself into a small seat, facing forward from the talons.

As the golden raptor flew toward their first challenge, a smaller raptor flew alongside. As birds of similar feather get together, the stranger asked in eagle speak, "I wish not to interrupt such a lovely one in high flight, but you seem to have what one may call 'a leftover' hanging on your leg."

Gustav did not speak as an eagle would speak; he just heard one side of the conversation. Staying motionless, he looked down at the visiting raptor with a very slight turn of his head. Not daring to take deep breath, his heart was pounding as he waited for Ariel's response. "You certainly are observant. There is a creature clinging to my leg. Thank you for noticing, and I will attend to this later. Goodbye."

Thinking loudly in conversation to his love, Gustav said, "Am I a leftover? You are saying that I am just a faux pas?" "My dear companion, I'm sure the great bird would have helped me remove this unsightly blemish if I had asked." If an eagle could laugh, Ariel laughed as she soared higher, with Gustav holding on for his dear life.

CHAPTER ELEVEN

A SEED IN NEED

The land beneath the duo unrolls in a patchwork panorama of small castles, farms, villages, and life as they crossed the great mountain and entered new lands. In their quiet thoughts, they heard a call of distress. The call grew louder as they realized that they were close to their first challenge and approaching a large farm. "Help me! They are going to bake me alive, then they will eat me."

Not knowing what else to do, Gustav called out and talked to that which was distressed. "Friend in distress, we hear you, tell us where you are, and we will find you." "Well, just don't take your time because I don't have much time for me and my family." The eagle spoke. "If you do not wish to bake, please hold your tongue and give us directions."

"Well, pardon me for asking. I'm being held captive in the small thatched-roof home with a large stake fence surrounding it and a monstrous dog. Please come soon." The eagle and the ferret both saw the house, the dog, and the owner of the house performing various chores around her abode. No one appeared in distress. "Whoever you are, where are you located at this house?" Gustav asked the strange new voice.

"I am a pumpkin seed, located in a pumpkin pie that is going to be baked very soon. It is a long story. If I don't get rescued, my progeny and I will be no more." "How very strange, this story you have told us." "Listen, sweet damsel, we can talk about all of this later. Now I need saving, and later we could talk, and you can find out how this affects both of you. I'll make it worth your while." The eagle landed on the limb of the tree that stood next to the house. Gustav scampered off the perch and began a search for the pie. He found the pie on a windowsill. He reached the windowsill, then he reached into the golden pie with his claws. It felt strange as he pawed through the liquid in search of the elusive and magical seed. He was not without the temptation to taste while he was searching. He found one seed among many and took a lick.

"This is pie is delicious. What a strange thing to leave in the pie. She must not be a very good cook to leave seeds in a delicious pie." Suddenly, they heard a little girl as she screamed, "Mommy, there's that big white rat tasting our pie." "A white rat indeed!" "I've been insulted." This was his thought as he put the seed in his mouth, clamped down tight, and ran for an exit. He was fast as he streaked along the windowsill. Just as he jumped off the edge, a large straw broom came crashing down on the pie. The pie dish and pumpkin flew all over with the impact of the broom. It was a wild, noisy commotion that came from the woman, who was a wife, mother, and not a very good pie maker. She hollered and screamed as she pursued the little white beast. She ran around to the outside of the house, calling out for all to hear:

"I'll kill that very little beast, if I can find it." In the large open area surrounding the house, Gustav found a tree stump. He clambered up the large platform and called, "Ariel, I need you now." As a young furry knight opened his little clawed hands in greeting to the great eagle, he called to her, "I'm ready if you are. Please hurry." As Gustav waited for his feathered love, he heard a barking dog. The woman of the house ran around the house, holding her broom and calling for the dog. Her children followed her in mock distress, with their own wild screams. The little ones appeared to be having great fun as the woman of the house saw the ferret appearing as the sacrificial lamb. He stood at the center of the tree stump and appeared to have no other place to go. "Where are you, Ariel?" pleaded the ferret as he reached for the sky.

"I'm on my way, my dear." The shadow of the bird flew over the irate pie maker. With openmouthed astonishment, the woman and her children stopped in their tracks as they watched a golden eagle swoop down and pick up the ferret. The woman then gathered her children. Trying to be calm, shrugging her shoulders, she told her children that nobody will believe this story. "Just tell them what you saw. Now embrace your children and take them back home to make another pie. By the way, I am a ferret, not a mangy rat, madam."

In openmouthed astonishment, the woman turned in a circle as if to break the spell. She then closed her eyes for a moment of meditation, then watched as the magical duo slowly rose in flight into the distant orange-hued sky. It was many years later that the woman still swore that the little white "rat" waved to her.

Later that evening, her husband returned from the market and saw the mess. He also noticed his wife's expression as she sat in front of their home, staring blankly in thought. He thought it better not to ask. Faint scattered lights twinkled below as the duo headed for roosting place. "Where are we going?" the seed pleaded. "A place of rest and a place to eat is what I need. This will also be a place of meditation," spoke Ariel. "What about me?" cried the magical kernel. "You will have another day of life." This said by the Bird, who appeared irritated at the impetuous magic seed.

"Into the beak of death go I, a magical rescuer of kingdoms, farms, and other souls in need," the seed lamented as it lay within the jaws of Gustav. "Shall we just plant you from here?" Gustav asked as they looked down upon the vastness of the various kingdoms since the fading light. "No, I'll be a good seed."

Within moments, they landed in a flutter of wings as Ariel found a place to roost. There was an audible sigh from all. Gustav had been holding the seed tightly as they reached the resting place. He then called Elizabeth in his thoughts. "What shall we do with this whining seed of so much magic?" She replied, "My, a little seed of so much magic, and it wants protection?"

The pumpkin seed spoke again in a more serious vein, "My dear rescuers, it has been many seasons since I did anything of magic. Since only one of us has the memories of our past, I will pass on a small history. Each season, one of my progeny tries to outgrow the others. It is a celebration of magic that occurred so long ago. It was a starlit sky; celebrations were happening, and transport was needed. A very nice lady turned one of my ancestors into a very lovely carriage. Like all good things, it only lasted for a few hours, but what a trip. Since then, one of us is able to do a good turn when needed. Somehow, I ended in that silly pie, but you were there to continue the celebration.

"Who are you, dear feminine, elfin voice?" asked the seed. "I am certainly not the godmother of a pumpkin seed," responded Elizabeth in a huff. She continued, "Gustav, please put down the seed, and I shall create a suitable home for it."

A chant began.

"Let us find a place to rest, a home to be, small to carry, to lift, to soar.

It is to save a kingdom and maybe much more.

So here we'll find a sack for the seed.

Make it light as a feather for a pumpkin in need.

Make it pretty, says this cute little fairy.

Make the outside smooth and the inside kind of hairy.

Enough of this silly chant make it so, make it now.

At the count of three, bring it here, make it wow."

A beautifully crafted satchel of very small proportion appeared as Gustav held it up for Ariel to see. Then they heard this voice from within the satchel. "Hey, it is dark in here, kind of warm and snuggly. In fact, it is hairy, but I like it." "It is most polite for one to say thank you." As Elizabeth chided the seed, the seed remarked, "Thank you, all."

The ferret picked up the satchel and found straps and slung over his shoulder. He then said for all to hear, "It is comfortable and very light. I could even keep a few tasty snacks within this sack." "Just don't forget that I am in here with your tasty snacks." The satchel had two straps for carrying. The ferret with his tiny claws easily placed both of these straps over his upper legs and around his chest. Then he ran with it firmly attached to his sleek little body.

Although the ferret chose to stand when meeting friends, he needed all four legs to run. "The workmanship is quite fine, Elizabeth," Gustav said as he ran with the sack firmly against his body. "I am leaving for now, Gustav. You may call for me anytime you have a question or need. Please remember that you will have me just for a little while. You and your love will then be on your own. I will be here to help you to adjust to your new stature and calling. Just imagine, from protector of kings to a rescuer of kingdoms, farms, and regular folk. Good night to the three of you, and may your tomorrows be filled with great adventure."

As Gustav curled into a small furry ball, he felt alone in the dark night. The coolness of the night penetrated his small body as he mourned the memory of his past life. It became a deafening silence until he heard and felt the light from a sweet elfin voice. "Take a deep, slow breath, my little friend. Now breathe out slowly and relax. Your love is above you, perched on this great tree. She too feels alone and mourns for the memories of her past. Good night, Ariel, Gustav. Sweet dreams to you both."

They said good night in unison, and both found sleep. As Gustav slept, he dreamed of knighthood and his sweet love. He found her in a beautiful forest beckoning to him. He reached for her; her lips were inviting as he drew close to a kiss. Then she opened her eyes, and he saw fear as she screamed. He awakened with a start and then heard the call of a night creature. As sleep returned, he dreamed of marvelous flight beneath his golden-feathered love.

Gustav awoke the next morning and had a craving for fruit, nuts, and other delicious tidbits he found around his temporary dwelling. He heard the voice of his sweet love, but her voice appeared stern and commanding. "Run to that tree stump, climb to the top, and greet me in loving embrace." He scampered to the top of the tree stump and watched for his love. Seeing her diving toward him, he closed his eyes and opened his little ferret arms for a morning embrace. The embrace was jarring and brief as he found his lifeline. He then heard her voice again and listened.

"Please open your eyes and look at where you were." Looking down, he saw another large animal as it recovered from a lunging effort to reach Gustav. The animal screamed a terrible howl as he looked up to the heavens and saw the eagle with the ferret attached. Pulling himself up, he wrapped himself as best he could around the great talon. Then he heard her again and listened. "You must be very careful on the ground, little ferret. My Pretty may be gone, but there are others who will gladly take her place. Please feel alert and alive and let us search for next challenge." Just then they heard the faint whiny voice of a pumpkin seed. "Hey, are we all right?"

After a brief flight, Ariel landed, and she asked Gustav to stand in front of her. She then reached down very carefully and gently clasped him, setting him up on the branch at her eye level. She then nudged him playfully. He appeared to be quivering in her presence. "I hear your thoughts and know that it is you. But in my ferret eyes, I stand in abject fear before a large golden raptor. Then you touch me with your beak, and the fur on my back rises then falls as in great undulating waves reflecting my total awe of your presence."

Ariel decided to try a new way of ferret travel. He would travel on her back, holding onto her feathered neck. Though no longer needed, the golden rope was placed around her body like a harness. This provided a solid way for Gustav to hang on during flight. The two, with the satchel, practiced many times until they became as one.

It was late evening when they all called it a beautiful day. After the last practice flight, Gustav left the satchel beneath them in the place where he had slept. As they conversed on the tree stump, a small creature had investigated the hole and found the satchel. Grasping it in his teeth, he took it and ran with it. As the small animal ran down a familiar trail, a great whirlwind of dust and wind stopped the animal in his tracks.

With small, round, very sad eyes, he looked up into the face of his possible demise. Then the great bird reached down and took the satchel and placed it on the ground beside the quivering rabbit. Then she spoke. "You, little morsel, have taken something of mine. You should be grateful that you're carrying a magical sack. I do not wish to spoil the charmed being within this container. You may leave, before I change my mind." Not to be asked twice and with fluid movement, the large furry rabbit slowly backed away, turned, and fled for his life. The creature found his family, but none believed him, but they were quite puzzled by the fact that he had turned white in his brief journey. It was a great story to pass on to his large posterity.

The small satchel was picked up by the ferret. The orange seed thought for all to hear: "I felt flight, are we moving again?" The female voice reassured the seed. "Orange, that's your name. Now as I crave pumpkin seed, I also search for a useful function that you may perform." "Oh my goodness, usefulness?" shouted the seed. "I feel a call to serve, and yes, it is very strong. Don't you feel it too? We must prepare for flight, Your Highness of the skies and billowing clouds. The voices of need are reaching into the depths of my being, even as a little seed. It's time to fly."

The eagle whispered in thought to the ferret: "Real or imagined, it's fascinating as to when fear will compel us to new and greater heights." With the satchel attached to the ferret and the ferret attached to the eagle, they flew. Multiple shades of grays, blues, and billowing puffs of white accented the cloud-strewn sky as they flew. It was in great quiet solitude as Ariel followed directions from the magical seed. In the grand constantly changing panorama, they listened for the call. Through the rushing of the wind, the seed was asked, "What is your purpose, and are we close to our first adventure?"

CHAPTER TWELVE

FIRST QUEST/LITTLE ELENA

"Oh good gracious," cried Orange. "Down below, I see little girl clinging to a windowsill a great distance above the hard earth. There is no one around to save her. Do you see her, Ariel?" "I see her, and we will dive to her rescue. Question: how are we going to save her?" "I will do what I do best. Please, quickly plant me beneath the little one, and I will perform great magic for you and especially for the child."

The rushing wind became as a scream upon the delicate ears of the ferret. His claws gripped the magic cord that held him to her feathered back. Ariel's wings were buffeted as she sped to the site to the rescue. The castle grew closer and closer as the trio plummeted toward the earth. Then Orange spoke up. "I've never been planted from this depth." Slowly, the great golden eagle extended her legs and talons as a means of breaking her speed and slowing her breathtaking descent. With her wings extended and with the graceful fanning motion, she landed just below the little girl. The little girl had been crying out for help, and yet not a soul was there to hear. The little girl in peril looked below as Gustav climbed off the bird and ran with the satchel to just below the crying girl. He then withdrew the seed and stuck it in the ground. Quickly, he climbed back aboard his feathered love, and with graceful strokes of her wings, they quickly looked for a place to watch. They found a high branch to watch and see what came next.

Within a very brief moment, the seed grew quickly to a pumpkin; it had expanded and expanded until it ballooned into an immense squash. With a grand explosion of the seeds, orange stuff, and internal pumpkin matter, the little girl was saved. When she fell, she landed upon the giant pumpkin that materialized magically beneath her. "Thank you, my poor pumpkin, for saving my life. I certainly have made a mess of you, and I am very sorry. My name is Elena. I think that I am going to be a good witch." The rescue party said not a word. It was quite a sight as there sat the young witch to be in the middle of a great pumpkin mess.

"Elena," called her mother, who was looking out the window from which the little girl had fallen. Looking down from the window, she saw her little girl. Elena's mother was crying and calling out her name as she raced through the castle and out the door. She then scooped her into her arms, checking for bruises and possible broken bones. As the woman began removing pumpkin parts, she backed away from the spot with the little girl holding her mother tightly. She looked up and then down the orange mess. She whispered to her, "Dear, you are protected, but by whom?" Putting the little girl down and taking her hand, she walked her through the great doors into the castle. The little girl with flowing red locks looked back over her shoulder and saw the bird. She waved as they entered the castle. Gustav and Ariel flew quickly down to the orange mess and asked, "Which one do we take little magic seed?" "Please, grab any one of them and place me in the sack before they return to clean up the mess."

As they rested on a large branch overlooking the castle, Ariel commented, "You mean to say that there are hundreds of you? I find it hard to deal with one of you," she said as she giggled to herself. "Unfortunately only one survives, and that's me—actually that's all of me. You take one, and the rest become just plain old pumpkin seeds." Gustav carefully placed the seed in the bag, and the trio took flight.

Ariel was hungry and left the other two to fish. She was gone for a while as Gustav sought out other seeds and a few berries. He felt full, and so he relaxed on the other side of the tree trunk. Then he heard his love's voice: "Please find the top of the tree trunk and open your arms." As he and his precious cargo were snatched from the spot, they heard the howl of the family dogs. The lord of the manor road approached, riding a large black stallion followed by a pack of very large hounds. The closer they got to the castle, the more excited the hounds became. They howled a greeting to their small family.

The mistress held her only child closely as they looked out the same window. The lord of the manor stopped as the excited pack examined the mess. As the wire-haired gray hounds searched through the orange-colored heap, the monarch looked up to his wife and back down to the mess. He saw his little girl still covered with pumpkin stuff. With a questioning look, he looked to his wife and mouthed the words, "What happened?" She shrugged her shoulders and stood there clutching her daughter and shaking her head. Though just a young girl, she was wise beyond her years. "Please, Mother, don't worry. All will be well. I'll be a good girl from now on."

Her mother smiled and kissed Elena on the forehead, pumpkin matter and all. After she had spoken to her mother, the large wire-haired gray hounds began to howl again in earnest. Her father tried to silence the dogs to no avail. He was becoming very agitated at not being able to control the hounds, and to add to the pandemonium, the stallion was even showing stress and began neighing in response to the howling.

Though held tightly by her mother, the young girl looked down upon this growing mournful chorus. "Okay!" she shouted in her little girl voice and immediately got the attention of the animals. Elena then held her forefinger to her lips in childish admonition. "Be still, my big babies." Within seconds, they quieted and peacefully lay down by the castle door. In openmouthed astonishment, her father just stood there, trying to understand what had just happened. The stallion also quieted and sauntered off to munch some grass. The father again looked up to his wife and motioned for her to come down.

CHAPTER THIRTEEN

GOODBYE, LITTLE GIRL

"A very powerful little witch or someone who knows how to love animals," said Gustav. The trio watched as the mother, the father, and the sweet little girl took a walk around the castle grounds. Because the eagle and the ferret, plus the seed, were good listeners, they heard the conversation. "We must stop the direction our little girl is headed. We must send her to the Order of the Little Sisters. They will know what to do with her," he said this as her mother cried out in earnest, "No, not there, please not with them," as she held her little girl tightly. Elena looked to her mom and gently patted her shoulder, saying, "It really won't be that bad, and I'll learn, grow, and become a very good girl."

The knight, his love, and the seed watched this family over the next few days as they packed and prepared to send their daughter away for education and protection. Though appearing serious and uncaring, the parents sent the little girl away with very great sadness. Elena was riding the stallion that her father had ridden. He had designed a smaller saddle that held her very well. Her parents held each other and wept openly as they waved goodbye. With her departure, the howl of the hounds echoed through the countryside as they escorted their little princess. Her entourage was followed by a small wagon with a few of the monarch's guards as protection.

Back at the castle, the father simply said, "We shall simply break the spell, my dear. The friar told me that the sisters were very good at taking the devil out of a child." This was no consolation to Elena's mother, as each night she would be found gazing out the window in the direction her little daughter had left. Each night she had visions of evil, cruel, and heartless villains. Her husband's words echoed and pierced her heart: "They will break her of her witching ways."

The raptor, the ferret, and the seed in a sack soared to great heights as they pursued the young woman. This quest was to follow and protect this wisp of a girl. She was a child of magic. The journey was long and tedious, but the child appeared quite content. She sang, holding on to the large horse's neck, often thinking thoughts of her home.

After several days and many hours traveling, she saw a large set of buildings surrounded by farms. She tried to imagine her tutors and looked for them as they approached the great doors of the main building. She was greatly surprised, as she stopped and dismounted to see a trio of what appeared to be silver haired ladies in black, hooded cloaks. The guards said goodbye to Elena and left her with the hounds and the stallion to be her companions.

She carefully dismounted and walked toward them. Then like the little princes she was, she gave a slight bow, saying, "Good evening, kindly ladies, my name is Elena, and I think that I am a witch." They stood for what seemed to be a very long time, looking at the little girl. Then in a protective formation, they surrounded her and, as a group, found the mother superior in her office. Elena very carefully curtseyed again to the grand lady who stood before her.

"Good evening, my child," said she, "I feel that your mother's heart has been wrenched from her soul in your departure. The sooner we help you change your direction, the sooner you will return home. You will go to your room, say your prayers, and then tomorrow very early, we will begin your instruction."

From sunrise to sunset, the young redheaded girl toiled. There were floors to scrub, windows to clean, and in fact, everything needed cleaning. She also studied five days a week: history, the arts, math, and she learned much more. She had several friends who she often convinced into assisting her in doing her chores. Even as a little girl, she had decided early that when she had a castle, lands, and possessions, she would never do housework again.

Through the following months, Gustav, Ariel, and Orange, as he was now called, flew over many realms and listened to many conversations.

After a few months, they returned to check on sweet Elena. She was a little taller and always appeared to be a loner. One dark and gloomy day, Elena was called into the mother superior's office. The head of the school looked up at young girl and, with tears in her eyes, asked sit to sit by her side. "My dear, your parents have been lost at sea. You are now the sole heir to your parents' lands and the castle.

"Your uncle is your protector, and he is the administrator of your estate. He has promised needed funds until you're ready to go home. I fear for your well-being, except that your uncle appears to be honest and very caring. What do you wish to do, my child?" "Mother, you and the sisters have been my family and had taught me great things of the world in the short time that I have lived here. You have secured me from my witching ways, and I will always appreciate the fact that you have allowed my hounds and horse to be here with me. I have been able to care for them and they for me. It is time to return to my castle. I have lost my parents—I will mourn for them and say a prayer of forgiveness for them having left me. The good thing was that they left me in such a wonderful place."

"Are you ready to leave?" "I must go, Mother. The time is far spent, and I must continue with the rest of my life." The magical trio had just arrived to the home of the Order of Little Sisters. They were surprised to see Elena as she rode through the gate of her temporary home, astride the marvelous black stallion. She was also escorted by the wire-haired gray hounds who howled in apparent jubilation. As she left, students and sisters all stood at the gate, waving white handkerchiefs and singing art songs of joy and remembrance. The Little Sisters could be seen wiping their crying eyes and comforting each other. Then, a short time later, students and sisters turned and reentered their home, shutting the gate behind them. Elena was entering a new chapter of life.

"Shall we follow her?" Ariel preened her feathers and looked around as she asked. Then she reached down to Gustav, playfully nudging him with her beak. This always seemed to disturb him, just a little bit, as he shuddered. She looked out and watched the young lady leaving. "I feel numerous possibilities. What shall we do?" "Here's to her safe journey," said the ferret knight. "Before we go anywhere, we must return home for a few days. I would like to see my parents, maybe Gretchen, and let us also find the king." They agreed, and early the next morning, they left. Gustav, Ariel, and Orange returned to the large Valley of their birth. Walking such a journey would have taken many days. In the air, the distance just melted away. They saw the granite peaks and knew they were home.

CHAPTER FOURTEEN

ADIEU, MOTHER AND FATHER

The telepathy was strong as they heard and rejoiced as they could hear voices of friends and loved ones. Gustav found his home of birth. There sat his parents under the shade of the first tree they ever planted. The farm appeared orderly; the crops were ready for harvest. As his mom and dad appeared somewhat fragile as he looked down upon them from a large tree, they stood up quickly and looked around when they heard the voice of their son.

"Mother, Father, I'm here. You look good, and it looks as though someone else is caring for the farm." "Where have you been, my boy?" his father said as his companion poked him in the ribs, and he grunted. "I am sorry. It's just such a great surprise and joy to hear you." "How is your lovely bride?" his mother asked. "I'm very well, thank you," said Ariel. "Oh, my dear, it's been a long time. Are you well? Are you?" It was then Gustav's father cleared his throat and then whispered to his love. His mother suddenly gasped and put her hands to her face saying, "You're spelled, and I'm daft."

"With tears flowing from her eyes, she first embraced her husband, and then choking with emotion, she called to Gustav, "I have prayed for you every night in hopes that I would hear your voice again. Now I have been rewarded with the sound of your voice. It is so good to hear your voice within my mind. My simple mind is sometimes easily confused, as I hear you, but I don't see you. Then my memory clears, and then I picture you both perfectly."

"It is good that we can see you. We appreciate your prayers. Though you cannot see us, we are in good health and, as always, in love. Please remember us because soon we must leave." His mother responded, "The time is also spent. There is little remaining for us. We will soon be as dust. Even though this may be our earthly finish, our spirits will fly on angel wings as we observe our conquering hero and his sweet companion. "You have made us proud, son. We love you." "Good night to you both. Ariel and I will return in the morning and tell you of our adventures."

For the next several days, it appeared as though his parents were really getting old. The hours they had together gently flowed, and quiet words of memories were spoken. With familiar intimacy, the bond of son to parents and daughter-in-law to parents with strengthened. Although the temptation to reveal their identity was there, they maintained the mystery of telepathy as the only way that they could communicate. Their conversations appeared to be very animated as they seemed to be talking to the sky. Those who are helping at the farm quietly watched the old folks for the next several days, as the old ones appeared happier than they had been for quite a while. Those who ran the farm tried not to watch the old couple. From a distance one day, the farmhands watched as the man and wife holding each other tightly appeared to be crying as they waved toward a very large bird.

"Well, nobody's going to believe us," one fellow commented. "I'm just glad the old man and his wife had some moments of joy, or so it seems. Let's just watch out for them." The farmhands checked often on the couple. One day, they had not heard from them for a while, so one of the fellows came to their home and knocked on their door. Hearing no response, he entered. The couple was found as though sleeping on their large bed. Indeed, they were asleep for the ages, as death quietly helped them leave their frail existence. There they lay in a loving embrace, with each appearing to hold, in their weathered hands, a feather. They were buried a short distance from their home beneath a large tree that overlooked their farm. As the few who knew the couple, including the king and queen, gathered beneath the tree to say their goodbyes. A large golden eagle flew over the tree and appeared to circle the farm. After this flyby, the large bird sailed slowly away and with a mournful scream appeared to say farewell.

As Gustav and Ariel flew toward the castle and away from his home of birth, he commented, "Thank you for allowing me the chance to remove a small token of our love from your sweet feathered body. I'm sure that tale will go around for many, many years." "I can still fly, and those two large feathers won't be missed. I would just like to be around to hear the many tall tales of what we have created."

As the magical duo circled the fortress of Angus, they saw a knight on horseback. Wearing a beautiful helmet with a single braid coursing down her back, she was immediately recognized. She suddenly halted her horse as she heard a familiar voice. "Gretchen, please stand and report." She responded, "Voices from my past, you must show yourself. Defend those wild tales I've heard of this knight of the realm. Speak to me, dear friend and bring music to my ears."

The music was indeed beautiful as she heard two voices in unison: "You're looking great, dear lady knight." Gretchen dismounted and quickly found a quiet spot. She laid her shield down and sat. She looked around for the source of the voices. "I hear you, dear friend, and your lady love. Share with me your tales, for I've missed you both. You caught me just in time, for I'm preparing to leave to become a soldier of fortune."

"A soldier of fortune, what riches do you seek?" asked her former friend and knight of the realm. "I am joining a large force, and we are going to try to stop or slow down a lumbering mass of humanity. This horde, as it is called, is devouring much land and riches of countries to the north. It is my opportunity to help, and it is my calling." One soldier of fortune and two voices from the past shared memories. "You must speak to your king," pleaded Gretchen. "With you disappearing, or shall I say, being spelled by the cat lady and with me seeking my fame and fortune, he is upset."

As she was speaking, a tall, well-muscled knight approached Gretchen and put his arm around her, and finally she said, "By the way, I will not be alone. This is my husband, Karl." The tall and handsome knight looked around with a questioning look on his face. "Who, my dear, are we talking to?" "Karl, the voices you hear are from a couple of old friends. Meet Gustav and Ariel." With that introduction, he promptly fainted dead away. Gretchen looked around and shrugged. "He'll be all right. He's actually a very brave and strong warrior. Ah, sweet mysteries of life, find this bear of a husband not immune to sudden changes of the climate. He has never believed my personal story of your change. Perhaps today, he will."

He was truly awake now as he spoke with new friends who heralded adventures that Gretchen could pass on to their children and their children's children. The square-jawed giant looked upon his love, the armored female with innocence of youth and passion. He then stood, looked about, and spoke: "Sir Gustav, I have doubted her all this time, and now you are here." He drew his sword and knelt, bowing his head.

"Please stand, Karl. We are all on equal ground, and welcome, the new friend to our very lonely existence." The two knights of different genders sat close together and spoke with her long-lost and new friends. It was a windy day, and it partially obscured the view of anyone looking out to where they sat. The hours seemed long, but laughter punctuated the stories as legends began with his historic embellishment. The two knights were silhouetted against the multicolored hues of the setting sun as they embraced; Gretchen once again called out to her telepathic hosts, "Be sure to speak with the king. Above all, stay well, knight of magic, and your sweet Ariel."

The next day before leaving, they spoke to Angus the King. He was glad to hear them and spoke of Gretchen. They told him that they had spoken with her and had met her husband, Karl. Though tired and aging quickly, the king was animated as he talked to the magical duet. They were in a quiet place, so no one observed his excitement of hearing the voices of old friend. They said goodbye, and the great golden eagle with its ferret rider carrying the magical seed rose in flight. Now they would search for Elena.

CHAPTER FIFTEEN

THE SPELLING OF ELENA

As Orange rested in the comfortable satchel, it heard the familiar husky voice of the great bird. "I may crave pumpkin seed now and then, but I desire to hear your crazy wit and humor even more. Entertain us in our flight, please." Into the cloudless sky flew the trio of travel and magic. It took many days of travel to get close to the call. While resting in the early morning, they saw a sign through the misty fog. A shooting star interrupted their solitude with a brief shower of brilliant colors. As a finale, the sparkling colors appeared to shower the countryside, causing dogs to howl, cows to moo, and the trio to watch and wonder.

"I feel forces that abound in this land that may have an effect on all of us and even our youthful Elena. She is no longer a little girl." Again, the sky was lit by many large showers of pyrotechnic magic and mayhem. They noticed in the field the young lady of flaming hair, and she too was mesmerized by the magic. The trio found a place to watch with joy, as Elena had been found. Though she was still very young, she demonstrated maturity as a traveler. The deafening silence after the early-morning pyrotechnics display reached the young girl as she watched the source of the bright display.

She could see a colorful wagon that stood alone, with small children chasing each other around the trees that surrounded the wagon. Then she saw adults sitting quietly and appearing to have conversation. There was an attraction that beckoned to her curiosity. She rode with great control astride her black stallion as they cautiously approached. Maybe was another family was calling to her or it was the shooting star that possessed her. Something was whispering to her, and she had to answer the call. The stallion appeared to hesitate and even balked at going toward camp.

Elena relaxed and embraced the horse's large neck as she said in a sweet tone, "Knight, be still, the hounds are close to us. All I need to do is call them. They will come and offer protection." The great horse still demonstrated a reluctance to move toward the wagon, but Elena was very persuasive in her ways. As the stallion and rider approached, her eyes were wide and alert to the danger. She listened as the camp appeared very silent.

The mistress of the camp placed her long thin fingers to her lips as Elena approached. "Hush, my children, for we had a visitor to greet us in this early morning. I hear coins in her purse, and she rides a great beast." Into the camp walked the stallion with his rider, who was now wearing a hooded cloak. She smiled, noticing the leader. They all appeared to smile with no emotion and slowly surrounded her as she entered the center of camp. "Greetings. I saw the camp and wish to join you."

The stallion snorted in alarm as the small crew tightened the circle around the duo. Elena padded his neck and whispered sweetly in his ear, and he quieted. She called and looked around to those who surrounded her, "Please move back from my horse. He is very sensitive to crowds, and the black Knight may rear in alarm." Then she heard the voice of the old woman. "Welcome. We're poor travelers who live off the land and entertain with magic and song.

"It will cost you to stay for just a little while. Stay and have a warm drink. We now require payment, for we will now take all of what you have, and that includes your horse. We will leave you with your life and a few meager possessions that you may carry. You may breakfast with us and nap, then you will leave before the sun is high in the sky."

"You, dear hag, purveyor of threats and dark magic, are most kind. I'll have to reconsider this gracious offer of food and protection." The old one whistled a shrill call, and all who surrounded her attempted to capture the young rider and the horse. The horse reared as the old one shouted for silence. "If you value that animal, you'll quiet him, or my archer will take the horse's life."

Elena pointed back beyond the circle and asked, "Is that your bowman?" They all looked back and saw that that person was flat on the ground with a hound at his throat. Then they noticed that the hound was not alone.

There were many hounds surrounding the camp. One hound stood next to the old one and snarled. Members of the camp were all herded to the center where their leader sat down and pondered their dilemma. "Peace, I pray, young woman. You have countered us, and you owe us nothing. What we have in meager possessions is yours, but please leave our children. This meager existence has hardened us, and we are without honor."

She shook her head and looked all around, especially at the children. "Your words are shallow and cheap as the trinkets you sell and the magic you perform. I wish to leave and shake up the soil of this camp from my boots." "No," shouted the gypsy as she hurled herself to the ground in front of the horse and rider. The stallion reared in alarm and barely missed trampling the thin ageless witch. "Do not curse me and my family in such a way. Leave us in peace. And I will give you a treasure that has been my family for generations."

"Let me see it first. I then will decide your fate." Above the scene sat Gustav, as he and Ariel pondered the radical change in little Elena. The old one brought out a large blanket shrouding a book. When the others saw what she had brought forth, they called out to her. With fear registering on their faces, she silenced them and called to the rider, "This is a book of spells, incantations, and other magical mayhem. They will bring you wealth, fame, fortune, or death, if misused. Study it and practice, practice, practice, and pray that you do not curse yourself to the fiery depths of the craft."

As the old one handed the book over to young girl, her thin, bony fingers appeared cold and lifeless as they held on to it us just a few more moments. Then, after briefly grasping Elena's hands, she released her grip and began backing away. The hag smiled with an almost deaths-head grin, cackling while bidding farewell. Her eyes appeared black and soulless. With a shrug of resignation, she turned her back, and all the others joined, not a one saying a word, as many of the group embraced.

Elena called the hounds as she remounted the great horse. They turned quickly and, in a fast trot, left the camp. She wanted to distance herself from this strange place. Looking back, she saw the blanket-covered package tied to her saddlebags. "I don't remember doing that," she said as she and her companions raced swiftly, stirring the low-hanging fog into turbulent seas.

Silently, the hounds ran through the ferns and grasses of the dark forest, keeping pace with Elena. She heard another rocket as it shot skyward. The young rider slowed her horse and then stopped, turned, and watched. The hounds appeared restless as the horse snorted with excitement. Finally, the hounds just sat and howled. They appeared to plead with her with their expressive dark eyes. They rested on the crest of the hill and watched below.

Looking down at the small camp, she noticed a cloud of darkness with swirling winds buffeting the small wagon as members of the camp were seen hanging on the trees and the wagon and crying out in fear. The old woman walked slowly to the remains of the campfire with her arms outstretched, as though calling out to something. The winds whipped around her and appeared to shake the ancient body like a small rag doll. Her vibrating form could be seen within the cloud; suddenly her movement stopped. A deathly scream could be heard as a flash of lightning engulfed her and a brilliant flame extinguished the witch. All was quiet as the others covered their heads and crying aloud, pleading their innocence. All of the others were then embraced by the maelstrom, and the camp disappeared. The area where they had camped was barren. The cloud appeared to hover, and streams of blackness reached as tentacles along the ground, appearing to search.

"It is time to leave this hellish place, Ariel," cried the ferret knight as he clung to the tiny rope and buried his face in her feathers as the winds buffeted them. She rose quickly to escape. They had lost sight of the young rider as they too sought to flee from this scene of terror. In the heights above the forest, the air was cold and clear, almost peaceful. They looked back and saw the churning mass of air begin to move. "That hellish demon will lead us to our Elena." The eagle turned about, and they followed the wrathful fury.

The soft soil of the trail muffled the impact of the great horse's hooves as they raced along the trail, away from the camp and the swirling dark cloud. The great stallion with his rider searched for distance to separate them from the scene. The hounds finally stopped; they could go no further as they howled and lay panting. The pack had found a small creek and sought to drink, with their tongues playing hide and seek between swallows. It was a small comic relief for their mistress. She knelt by each one and gave care. She caressed their ears and heads and proceeded to carefully check their paws for cuts and bruises. As each hound was examined, their mistress moved to the next and then to the last. She finished caring for her small entourage of wire-haired beasts. She found a rock to sit upon, and all received a group hug with slobbery licks of affection. The great black horse snorted and nodded, as if in agreement. She also gave care to the horse, and all were quiet for a moment.

Gustav and Ariel were following the violent funnel cloud from a distance. The dark vortex still sought the young girl. "I'm afraid for her and what she may uncover within that bundle." "Yes, my little knight, I felt strangeness deep within my feathered body. Let us watch, pray, and hope that this does not lead her into a dark place." Gustav felt chilled as he held to her talons. He then climbed to his feathered saddle and found warmth.

Miles from the searchers, the young one rested. She removed the bundle and felt coldness through the wrapping. Finding a convenient stump, she laid the bundle down and carefully exposed the large leather-bound book. She heard the stallion and looked at him; he appeared to be shaking his head, pawing the ground, and snorting as if disagreeing. She ignored him and slowly opened the book. "I'm just looking." She gazed dreamily into the distance and pondered a dream.

"Think of having wealth, and power with just simple spells." She stopped in midsentence as she read and then quietly said, "Oh." She slowly took a deep breath and then read aloud a small printed word. "According to this, I must be careful, for there are dire consequences if the spell is misused." The horse nodded vigorously in affirmation. Gently holding the horse's head, she looked into his beautiful face. "Well, my bright and precocious horse, I'm only going to look at one spell, and I'll be very, very careful.

Then, turning the weathered pages, she stopped and looked up, saying, "Here, this is one that I seek. To spell for love. I have not love, but I will soon seek one. And with me being so forward and precocious, maybe I just need bewitching words." Knight still appeared anxious as he continued to breathe heavily. She continued to read and also try to calm the stallion with gentle strokes to his head. "Please be still, my great friend. If I do not feel comfortable with this, it will not be used." She pulled the cloaked hood over her head and continued to read, quietly whispering and repeating the words until it was in her memory. A sound was heard, an unearthly whistling, a strange wind. She looked up and in distance; she saw that it had found her.

She said nothing, standing up after again covering the old leather-bound book of incantations and then tightly strapped in to the saddle. She then whistled for the hounds to gather; mounting the black horse, she sought a path to escape. The cloud approached, searching with dark appendages, flashes of lightning, and deep rumbling thunder. It paused for a moment and then moved toward the small group.

She watched as the funnel approached, uprooting trees and bushes as the demonic cyclone found the keeper of the book. She dismounted and walked away from her steed and the hounds. Crying, she walked back to Knight and slapped his flanks, sending him and the hounds into the forest away from her. She then knelt, carefully laying down the blanket with the old book placed in its center. She looked up and faced the vortex, calling, "Here is the keeper of spells and incantations. It has not been harmed. If you seek justice, take me, not my friends, for they have done nothing except to protect me."

The air became charged around Elena as she felt that this was her last moment of life. There was a blinding flash and the supplicant was thrown up in the air, and she landed in the soft soil away from the book, still and silent. The book was taken up by the funnel and slowly swirling demon moved away. It could now be seen above the forest, no longer uprooting trees or bushes. In a brilliant flash, it disappeared.

Gustav and Ariel, though buffeted by the winds, were not injured. They looked down and saw as she lay quiet upon the soft earth. "Please be alive, awake, and face a new day." The golden eagle soared and circled above this spot in the forest. "Can I, only a seed, help?" As they flew closer and watched, the seed heard a response, "Just keep her in your thoughts." The young spelled knight clinched tight to the tiny rope that encircled his love and pleaded for Elena to be alive and to awaken.

She slowly awakened with the soft prodding of an equine snout and the gentle drooling kisses of the wire-haired gray hounds. Arising, she looked around and saw the path of the wind which had found her and the book. There was no wind, no cloud, just anxious friends that closed around her. Slowly, she got to her feet, and the hounds howled in apparent jubilation. The great black stallion pranced about, kicking up his rear legs in an equine dance of joy.

They finally settled down and waited her next decision. She found some bits of food in her saddlebag and ate sparingly. Holding the reins of her great friend, she slowly walked down the trail. A few miles from her encounter, she found a place to camp with water and grass. "My gray friends, I believe you need to find your own food."

After scavenging for food, they all gathered again for the night and slept. Awakening the next morning, she looked around and realized that her surroundings were becoming familiar. The castle, housing her uncle and forgotten memories, was near, and soon a new chapter of her life would begin. Above her, she heard the great call of an eagle. Looking up, she saw the golden-feathered bird of prey. The young girl also noticed a strange white patch that lay upon the eagle's back.

"Such a beautiful corsair of the sky! What a sight it must be to command such a view of the earth." "Yes, it is marvelous up in the clouds to view life and to see you." In just a quick moment of time, she fainted after hearing the thoughtful comment. She awoke sometime later and slowly looked around for the one whose voice she heard. "Please let me know who you are and show yourself."

The sounds around her were of the forest, friends, and nothing more. "Speak to me when you can." She looked around and, smiling sought nourishment for her and her friends. She knelt by a small stream and splashed the cold liquid onto her face. Then she playfully splashed several of the hounds as they drank beside her. She finally stood, and after securing her meager possessions on the saddle, she mounted her steed, and the small group of friends sought the trail. As she looked ahead, she again saw the great raptor as it appeared to be gliding above the surface of a small lake. Then its talons were seen to reach into the silver surface, and when they reappeared, the eagle was grasping a good-sized fish.

"What a catch! That looks delicious, fisher of the waters." Then a strange thing happened. As the bird flew her over with its catch of the morning, it appeared to drop it very close to the mounted rider. She stared at the catch as it bounced upon the ground. The hounds looked at her and then to the fish as it lay quietly. They backed away and waited for her to dismount. *I am hungry*, she thought. "I think a campfire would be in order." She looked up and saw the raptor had caught another fish. This time, it appeared to fly off to an open area near the top of a small knoll. She prepared her fish, and then it was cooked. As she ate each morsel with relish, she quietly thanked her benefactor. "You're very welcome," said the voice.

"I am beginning to like fish, Ariel, although it is not as tasty as the one being cooked by the young one." "Children, are you near?" The ferret and the golden eagle looked around for the source of the calling. "You know where we are, Elizabeth. Have we done something wrong?" "No, dear knight, I thought that it was time to talk both about your future and Elena's. You and your winged love have accomplished so much in so little time.

"Now, you need to back away and observe her without so much talk. I believe that she feels that you are part of the spell, and we can't have her thinking this. You must say adieu for a time and let her find her way. We all need freedom to choose our path. Her path may be fraught with danger or even sadness, but it must be her choice."

"I feel as though a parent may, as I anguish over this young one." This was a comment by the raptor, as she watched the mounted rider and her hounds begin their next journey. She carefully bent over and gave a playful nudge to her knight in furry armor. "I feel the same." Gustav stroked the feathers of his partner and then climbed back aboard as she stretched her wings in preparation for flight.

Elizabeth stayed with them in their thoughts as they lifted up and away from the small patch of open forest, and together they pursued the billowing clouds. After a few hours traveling, Elena dismounted and gazed upon a lone mountain peak. As she pondered her next move, the spell came to her as a dark forbidden thought. Startled, she looked fearfully around for the dark clouds.

The hounds appeared to feel her anxiousness, and the horse came near and stood to his side as if to protect. She forced the incantation out of her conscious mind and back into the dark recesses of her memory. She knew it would not go away and that the loving spell could be recalled by simple thought or a gentle touch. A short time later, she arrived at the top of another small hill. In the distance, she saw her home of birth. As she reached the open gate, she looked in and saw the tower from which she fell and was saved. Her uncle was approaching as she dismounted. He was using a cane to help with his limp and with hair of glistening white; she knew aging had found him. One of his guards followed closely to assist if needed. With cane in hand, he approached his young niece, and they embraced. With tears flowing freely, he said, "Oh, my dear young one, I have continued to live for this moment." He pointed to a bench; with hounds in tow, they rested and talked.

Though her uncle had appeared venerable since she last saw him, he still possessed wit, wisdom, and the knowledge of strange facts. He spoke with sorrow of the passing of his wife. He led Elena around the small castle, pointing to her new residence and to a possible location for the kennel for her hounds. Her uncle, Charles, spoke to her at great length about their neighbors, the country, and finding a mate. "As soon as you're ready," he commented, "let us have a ball, and you can meet all of the eligible bachelors in the country." Though she was still quite young, she agreed, and they began planning.

CHAPTER SIXTEEN

LOVE SPELLED

Though this castle was nothing on the order of that owned by King Angus, it was still spacious and well fortified. It even had a royal carriage that could be pulled by four magnificent stallions. Elena was impressed by the castle and especially the carriage. Her uncle allowed her free rein to do whatever she pleased in improving the castle. She took it to heart by promptly having the carriage painted black.

The castle was resplendent with banners, lanterns, and a small orchestra. Those who were invited were ushered into the grand ballroom. There were refreshments, and laughter abounded. Elena made her entrance in a beautiful gown of shimmering silk and lace. She noted one young man who caught her fancy. Unseen by anyone, she stepped into a small alcove and whispered those words of the love spell. There appeared to be a sudden rush of air; the lights flickered, and everyone looked around for the cause. Elena walked to the center of the ballroom, and then turning to a special gentleman, she motioned to him. He looked around to those he was talking to, and everyone else was looking at him. He shrugged his shoulders. Looking at Elena, he pointed to himself and asked, "Who, me?" She slowly nodded her head, and he walked to her. As soon as they met, they embraced, and he was hers. Others joined in the dancing, and they gave a wide berth to the young couple.

Late into the night, holding her ever so gently, he lifted her high and looked up to her bewitching smile. As everyone was preparing to leave, he called for silence. "We have decided to marry and soon." There was a gasp from the revelers as they marveled at this sudden change of events. Her uncle was surprised also, but with a twinkle in his eye, he congratulated the two lovebirds. Little did he know that change was coming, and he would not be there to enjoy.

"I believe there is witching magic within those walls," this said was said by the ferret as Gustav and Ariel watched this sudden change. "I'm afraid you're right, my furry love. I wonder if Elizabeth is watching." They listened, and no one answered. They found a quiet place in the forest a small distance from the castle, and they rested for the night, hoping for a better morning.

Somewhat distracting from the joy of this strange match was the sudden death of her uncle. Uncle Charles had not been well, and the strain of arranging the ball and visiting with neighbors was too much. He was found asleep with the ages in his grand bedroom, clutching a pillow embroidered with his wife's name. He was buried in the hill that overlooked his home. Elena wasted no time, as she arranged a funeral and then announced the wedding within days of each other.

The two observers of the so-called witching ways were greeted by a small elfin voice, "Well, my children, here is another nice challenge for you two. This is one time you're going to have to just watch." They watched as the next days swirled about, culminating in the celebration with many laughing and shouting joyously. One could hear words like *love, marriage,* and *offspring.* Gustav and Ariel watched the special couple walking alone, away from the castle. He kissed her with passion, and then they walked back to the castle, enjoying the accolades of all who saw them.

As they were walking back to the entrance, Elena looked back to the forest and waved. He asked, "Who was that, Robin Hood?" She just shook her head, saying, "No, just some tiny folks that seem to want to change the world." She then pointed to where she waved. "I know who you are, and you will change nothing." The new monarch looked at the forest and looked at her, then shrugged, escorting his new bride back to the castle and the wedding chambers. For all records, the young groom was nephew to Charles. He was a delightful, fun-loving man who loved taking the black carriage out on the country roads, with the grand horses pulling with all their might.

Since the magical wedding, there had been much new construction in the castle. There was a grand hall and the large open courtyard within the castle walls. The great hall was used for parties, but it was unusual for its decor. There were the tapestries hanging from the walls and banners of heraldry displaying noble birthright. But the strangest part of the decor was the gargoyles that appeared to watch, and they were in the form of the mistress's hounds.

As with many gargoyles, if one were to stare at them long enough, you may imagine an ear twitch or head move slightly. The furry white knight and his partner perched unseen by an open window. "The gargoyles are so lifelike, and it doesn't help to see the real hounds moving between their stone counterparts." "Those hounds have changed, haven't they, Ariel? They both agreed that something was going on in the castle, but tonight they watched a handsome couple as he appeared very much in love.

Ariel and Gustav watched from a distance the castle and all the goings-on within and without the walls. It was a short time later when it was noticed that Matthew had not been seen for days. The youthful red-haired wench of the castle tried to defuse any rumors or gossip by trying to socialize with the surrounding monarchies.

She had visitors from time to time, and on one on unfortunate day, she had chanced upon a few gossips who were asking, "Where is Matthew?" A terrible scream issued from this young mistress of the castle, and she shouted, "I will not put up with such unkind rumors. My husband is away, and I am the mistress of this castle. Your visit is over." And with that, she clapped her hands once, and immediately twelve hounds appeared through hidden panel in the wall. They harmed no one as they walked through the crowd. They surrounded Elena, and facing out, they appeared in a lion-like pose. These great hounds appeared to be smiling, but this illusion was not seen by the crowd. They only saw and felt the intimidating presence of her pets.

With icy coldness, she forced a smile and looked at the small group and said, "You have fifteen minutes to vacate my castle. After that, I shall release the hounds to play with you. Snapping her fingers once, the hounds set up in unison. As they were leaving, one of the visitors was heard to say, "I wager that those were not the only tricks known by any hounds." The companion responded, "You wish to stay and test your theory with those noble beasts?" She shook her head and a carriage was quickly found, and the visitors left.

It was a cold night as one of the carriages was seen leaving Elena's castle. There were beams of the lantern light that struggled to the darkness to show the way to the twists and turns of the main road leading from Elena's castle. The lady within was nestled in the arms of her love and said, "What strange and frightening behavior of the mistress of this castle." He nodded in agreement and said, "Indeed, my love, we must keep an eye on this Elena."

During the following months, as Gustav and Ariel watched, Elena's frenzy continued. She began collecting old debts and taking over properties around her castle that had previously been given away by Matthew. She did this in lieu of unpaid debts. She began taking the oldest daughter of many of the families as a payment of debt to become indentured servants. Her personal militia grew to several dozen hooded mounted soldiers.

As the hounds slept and her guards stood in the watchful stupor, she dreamed. In her dream, she stood before a mirror. She saw the old hag who had given her the book. As she looked, the old one vanished, and in her place, there stood Elena. "I am bewitched," she began crying. "I have spelled my knight to keep his love, and I have insured my loneliness." She wept.

It all of this turmoil, life continues within the walls of the Elena's castle. Two unofficial members of report could be seen running like king's warriors. They were very fast, with quickness, speed, and agility. We have learned this from the father and he and his father and from other ancestors. They were sleek and gray, what should one could call castle cats.

CHAPTER SEVENTEEN

WHERE IS MY LOVE?

"For hundreds of years, cats were known for good and evil. It was known in some circles as the 'squash you all flat' theory. It sounds rather silly, but young cats were taught this art of survival. They dodged, ran, and tried not be squashed all flat. They have to do this with all of the hounds, guards, and horses about. Maybe through these cats, we will find the master of the house, Sir Matthew." said Elizabeth, as she gave a brief history of the cats.

Gustav commented, "Why don't I go down and follow these cats?" As thoughts go, there was a loud exclamation. "Wait a minute, my young knight. I know you are brave, but you still need to be cautious." The ferret knight shook his head and commented, "Boy, Elizabeth, you can sure shout. Please lower the volume. I will be careful, and I always have Ariel to protect me." "Just how can I, in all my feathered presence, follow you and those house cats?" He scratched his furry body and pondered. "You'll find a way, my beautiful raptor of the skies."

He dismounted from his love onto one of the castle walls and then entered a convenient window. He heard many sounds of life, including the hounds. As he scampered down through the halls, he spotted a cat and decided to follow it. As Gustav followed, he noted that it was a noble Persian cat. They were known for their fine hair and also for continued grooming. This cat was no different, as it stopped to survey its surroundings and clean often. Gustav had no trouble following the young cat through the halls and down the stairs.

He was so intent on the pursuit that he failed to notice that they had entered a small room. It looked like a small place of residence. The gray feline stopped and looked from left to right within the small room. Slowly, the beautiful cat's tail stopped moving. A soft guttural yowl was heard, and then Gustav heard numerous answers within the room. The cat slowly turned and looked directly at Gustav. It was then that he noticed that they were not alone. Up on the ledges rested several more of the felines as they looked down on the white ferret with hungry eyes. "I wish you could talk because then you would know that I am here to find the master of the castle." There was no response except that the gray Persian was now approaching the knight with cautious steps.

Gustav stood straight and tall as the gray cat slinked around him slowly. It sniffed close to him, never touching him. It came to his front and faced him with the pose of a leader, as the others joined him. "My name is Gustav, and we are here to help." They did not respond, but just then, he heard a welcome voice, "Let me see what I can do for you, brave knight." She spoke, or should we say, meowed. They all jumped up in unison and howled. Hissing and arching their backs, they backed away from Gustav. He heard another softer, gentler call to the cats, and they all appeared to relax, grooming, growling softly as they looked to the center of their attention.

"You speak, and I will do my best to interpret your words in cat." He stood straighter now and walked among these gray mousers. He carefully caressed the face of each, and they reacted with soft, guttural growls that vibrated within their bodies. "I hope those are friendly growls." He heard a very hearty laugh from Elizabeth. "They are what is called purring, young one. They know where Matthew is located, and I believe that they will lead you there. You must be very careful because of the hounds, the guards, and especially the Lady Elena. She will recognize your intent and will do whatever it takes to prevent your interference." He sat down next to the leader of the cats and rested. "I wish Ariel were here. I may need it quick escape if I am found." As a group, the cats turned, and with their long furry tails waving leisurely, they began to search.

Every so often, they could hear others walking the halls. It could be the guards, the hounds, or it could be the Mistress Elena. Gustav scampered along the many ledges and nooks found along the great hallways. Suddenly, they all stopped and quickly found a small recess in the wall. Gustav huddled together with an assortment of gray cats, and they waited in silence. Just as he was going to leave their little hideaway, a squad of tall female guards walked past. Following this squad was a group of the wire-haired hounds. As soon as they passed, Gustav said his companions continued their search. Soon, they came to a large metal door that had a small barred window.

CHAPTER EIGHTEEN
THE KING IS FOUND

The felines pawed the bottom of this great door and meowed softly. Gustav found purchase, and finding his way to the window, he peered inside. There within the cell, lighted by a flickering candle, stood the master of the house. The young man appeared dazed, yet he had that special regal look. As Gustav watched the young man, he tried communicating, but to no avail. "We will try to help you, Matthew. Ta-ta for now."

The cats looked up to the ferret and, with soft mewing, started to find their way out. They moved quickly, this time with an apparent sense of urgency. They were ground level, and all stopped, pausing at an open window. He got to the window and looked down at his guides and called out in thought, "We will find a way to help the small kingdom. Please be careful." Looking out of the window, he looked around for escape route. The hounds could be heard from another side of the castle. Then he called to the raptor, "I am out, and I am ready for pickup. I see a tree stump just a few hops away, and I'm going for the run."

"You have been turned into a rabbit?" He heard this giggling response from his love. "I think that I'm faster than a rabbit, and I have smaller ears. Please watch for me. I hear the hounds." The hounds could be heard, and they had his scent. It was a race for his life. As he caught sight of the stump, the hounds saw him and all began baying as though on the hunt they were. Gustav quickly found the top of the stump and, with open arms, greeted his love as she quickly grabbed him just as the lead hound leaped that the fleeing duo. "That, my dear, was just a little too close for comfort. Thank you for being so prompt." As they circled the castle, they saw the mistress of the manor looking up at them and laughing.

CHAPTER NINETEEN

NEIGHBOR TO THE RESCUE

"Thank you, Elizabeth. We certainly have our hands, or claws and talons, full." As they flew over the land, they noticed another castle just over a small rise. It was a modest yet well-kept fortress. They too had farms surrounding the small fortress. Up on the tallest of the ramparts could be seen a young couple in a thoughtful embrace. "Let us listen and see if they can help." This said of the golden bird of prey as she and her close companion circled high above.

Stephen and his bride, Constance, appeared to marvel at the high flyers. "Maybe that is a sign, my dear. Such is a beautiful sight to lighten our minds as we think of Elena. We must help her find herself and her husband, Matthew." Stephen and his queen were blessed with a young son, Eric. He was precocious, and though his parents tried to ignore it, the young heir to their throne claimed to speak to animals. He could often be found trying to converse with farm animals, equine charges of the castle, and even the feline mousers of the realm. It was usually a one-sided conversation, but you couldn't fault the young fellow for trying.

Eric felt that if he continued to make an effort to communicate with animals, sooner or later, success would be his. Though they didn't talk back, many of his conversations ended with the more intelligent members of the animal kingdom responding in positive ways. His personal mount always responded to voice commands from him. Though he was in his early teens, he was known to be one of the great horsemen of the area. Occasionally, when he awoke in the early hours, it seemed to him that many animals were waiting for his morning greeting.

One morning, he noticed his personal favorite, a noble cat of Persian ancestry. As the gray feline was grooming at the foot of his bed. He greeted it. "Well, my fine feline, what have you been up to?" The animal meowed softly and suddenly turned toward the window. He arched his back and began hissing and acting very strange. Erick looked back toward the window and saw a white weasel type of animal standing on his back legs and waving to him. "You are Eric, noble son of Stephen and Constance, correct?" The young man stared at this strange vision in openmouthed astonishment and said, "I think that is me."

"You, my young friend, are blessed with a good listening ear. Especially since you try very hard to communicate with members of the animal kingdom. May I introduce myself? I am Gustav, and the beautiful golden raptor you see flying above is my companion, Ariel. Though we were spelled by a wicked witch, our lives are dedicated to service for our countrymen. Even as a ferret, I, and my feathered mate, search for missions to help others in distress. You, Eric, can help us on the next mission—that task being to help the Mistress Elena and hopefully her husband, Matthew."

"This is the first time in all my one-sided conversations with animals that I have heard a response. I now have a very large headache, and I think I need to take a royal nap." "Young Eric, please rest for a moment, but note that you have had many responses from your conversations with animals. They may not speak, but they respond positively to your love and caring for lesser beings."

Gustav waved goodbye to the young man and found his way out of the castle. Eric took a short nap and then awakening with a start, shouted, "I believe you. What can I do?" His mother quickly came into his room and noticed her son at the window, again shouting for Gustav. "Who, pray tell, is Gustav, and why are you shouting for him? He turned slowly and, with a sheepish grin, looked at his mother. "A visiting animal was speaking to me, and his name is Gustav. He wants my help in saving Mistress Elena and her husband, Matthew."

The young princess of royal beauty looked at her son and motioned him to sit with her on the edge of the bed. She put her arm around him, saying, "You must be careful with such claims. Witches have been imprisoned, hung, or just chased out of the country for talk such as yours." He looked at her and then turned toward the window. With tears in his eyes, he continued looking out. "I wish not to be hung, imprisoned, or to bring any discredit to our family. The problem is, I know it is true, and I feel strongly that I must help to free the mistress and find her husband."

His mother nodded in affirmation and whispered to him, "This will be our secret. No one, except your father, may know of your conversations." He nodded in agreement, and they both looked out the window and watched the high-flying ferret knight. "What a marvelous sight, and it is a very strange day." He agreed. She left the boy, and he waited for further conversations.

That evening, after dinner, young Stephen, his father, and his mother watched as moisture-laden air and all its turbulence approached. Rolling thunder reverberated through the Valley, introducing violent lightning flashes. A curtain of rain was dancing toward them as they noticed the shimmering, dancing lights appearing to break through the wall of water. This was an announcement of the approach of a large black carriage pulled by four dark stallions.

At the reins of this carriage, with her hair waving into the darkness and the wind dancing with her gown, was Lady Elena. The hounds led this procession with the mounted rider, covering her flanks, as others scouted to the rear of this procession. Stephen, his bride, and his young son Eric, watched as though the demons from hell had appeared to arrive. To add to the chaos, a single rocket burst above them, adding to the pandemonium of hard rain and lightning flashes. Stephen raised his fist in anger and shouted to the winds, "Leave your witching ways at your own doorstep. We will not be intimidated." As the storm subsided, the rains following did nothing to diminish the preceding intimidating demonstration. All residents throughout this land were awake now and fearful of what may happen to them. Later, in the early morning hours, another rocket burst announced the wench's return to her home. "All of our land is at risk the longer she stays in power." This said by Stephen as he escorted his queen and son to their bedrooms.

Later that morning, as Eric rested, he watched as the golden raptor landed on his windowsill and the ferret knight dismounted and greeted him. "My young friend, it is time for your help. If you will, we need you to go near Elena's castle." The young fellow walked toward the window, scratching his head and slowly shaking his blond hair. "Gustav, I have never done anything of that sort. To challenge such a woman borders, I believe, on insanity. I don't think my parents would approve. Do you really think that I can affect any change or save her husband? I barely have a few whiskers on my face, and I can ride a horse. I'm quite clumsy, and I barely speak English, which is our common language." He heard a quiet laugh, and then Ariel spoke, "You are an heir to the throne, a privileged lad with great potential. You are also speaking through your mind to an eagle and weasel." Then Young Eric heard a gasp. "I am not a weasel! I am a ferret, and a very brave one, if you will."

Eric began to laugh and then scratched his meager chin whiskers. "You sound like a married couple, maybe even like my mother and father." "We are partners and companions for the ages. Though we are not as a married couple, we love each other, and we have much to do." Eric watched as the young ferret reached over and appeared to lovingly touch the talons of the great raptor.

A tiny voice was heard by young Eric. "What am I going to do in all of this?" The young man looked around and under his bed. "Okay, there is a third member of this strange, challenging group. Who are you, tiny whiny voice?" He heard the reply, "Whiny, tiny? I, young lad, am the great and powerful Orange." Eric sat on the edge of his bed and, folding his arms, looked at the ferret knight. "What is an orange?" "Take heart, dear boy," so spoke the Raptor. "May I introduce you to Orange, the pumpkin seed of very small stature?" All heard a sigh. "Why's everybody always picking on me? Yes, my young Eric, I am a pumpkin seed with magical properties. It was just a few seasons ago that I saved the young woman, Elena. Now we are here to save her again."

The young man looked at the ferret and then the eagle, saying, "It's about time I grow up, and I am ready if you are." Then the young fellow found a wooden bench and dragged it over to the window. "This is quite strange. Usually when I talk to animals, they don't they say a word. Now I'm having conversation with a beautiful eagle, a ferret, and, of course, a pumpkin seed. Where do we go from here?" He watched as the young ferret appeared to stroke his tiny chin with his claw. Then the white knight looked up to the eagle, and she looked down to him. "I think the first thing you need is a horse. Her castle is still a distance away. When can you find a horse, young Eric?" "I'll have to ask my mother."

"Let's say, at sunrise, we will be off." The young rider of eagles climbed aboard his sweet, and they began to leave. "We will see you soon." Eric saw them ascend into the clouds, and then he turned and thought to himself, "What am I doing?" He heard the voice again, "You will be just fine, my lad." Eric found his mother in the grand room, and together they walked out in the cool air and found a bench. "You may try to observe and even locate Sir Matthew, but try your best not to confront Lady Elena." His father found a short sword that appeared rather a long on Eric's rather short frame. He looked at his young son and said, "You're good with the sword, but you will be challenged by dark magic. You are quick, and you think well. I give you a father's blessing to stay safe and be successful."

His father put his arm around his queen and his son, and before he walked back to the castle, he looked in the eyes of his son and said, "I love you." His mother looked at him and, pointing to an old war horse, said, "There is your horse. Treat him well, and he will not fail you." She walked over to the great white stallion of years and spoke to him, "My great friend, you and I have never done such a thing as this supposed grand rescue. We have nothing to fear, for we are led by a very smart white weasel, I mean, ferret, and a beautiful golden eagle. They both talk to me, and they sound very intelligent. Both talk to me." The horse snorted and appeared to nod in affirmation of the conversation. "Please, great steed, do not talk to me. I will ascertain your needs." With that, he found a rope halter that had been carefully crafted by one who had cared for all the animals in the castle. He then found the leather saddle and blanket that went underneath. He set them aside and then reentered the living area to gather other provisions.

CHAPTER TWENTY

TO THE RESCUE

There was a chill in the air as Eric gathered his supplies. He rolled up his bedding and extra provisions within a large oilcloth. He found his mount and put on the halter and the saddle. He then tied his bundle of provisions to the back of the saddle. His parents were watching and marveling at how well he prepared for this very dangerous adventure. His father called out to him as he was riding away from the castle, "Take care, son, and don't antagonize the witch. Find Sir Matthew." He waved goodbye in a nonchalant way and headed down the well-worn trail.

There was a low-hanging fog, which parted as he traveled forward. The fluffy white sea of cool mist closed behind him. As the distance increased, he appeared to disappear, and all his parents saw were billowing puffs of fog that appeared to mark his way. His father quietly thought, "Be safe, my son. Return to us soon."

Eric felt a warm glow course through his soul, and he knew he would be watched over. He had a general idea where Elena's castle was located. As the sun broke through the clouds, he found a reference point to follow. They came to a small creek, and he decided to rest a moment. His horse drank and found some grass nearby. "We are following, young Eric." This came from the ferret, Gustav. As the fog continued to disperse, he looked ahead and spotted the raptor far above. He traveled for many miles, and during the afternoon, he decided to camp for the night. "You should see her castle by tomorrow, midday." "Thank you, Gustav. Should I do any preparation before I find the castle?"

"You have provisions and an attitude of service. When you observe tomorrow, it will come to you as to how to approach Elena's fortress. Eric heard a thundering sound coming near, and he decided to find shelter in a grove of trees. He dismounted and tried quieting the horse. The large white stallion appeared nervous, and with gentle pats and soft words, his mount quieted just as the black carriage with its entourage came barreling past him. As they passed, he saw Elena look out toward his hiding place, and she pulled all to a sudden stop. "I smell a boy in the woods. You have come to visit me, how nice. You can join my husband in the royal suite and dine with the cats and rats."

She cracked her whip, and the four horses started up. The guards in strict attention stared straight ahead, and then with her command, they continued forward. The group of hounds that had been following her stopped, sniffing the air as in search; they began to approach the woods. They made no noise as they came toward his location. They were snarling with a low, guttural, unnatural rumbling from within their wire-haired frames. Suddenly, from the sky came a scream of an eagle. It swooped low over the heads of the dogs, and after briefly trying to jump up and catch the bird, they retreated.

Looking toward the woods, they all gave a quick bark and turned to catch up with their mistress. They howled as they ran toward the fleeing carriage. The sound echoed of their mournful wails through the land. "What a daring attack. Are you okay, Gustav?" "Yes, we are well but somewhat winded by that dive from above."

Eric too was winded and very anxious as he stood resting his head on his horse. He sighed, looking toward the last of the hounds as they departed. "Well, that went well. There goes the surprise element of our adventure." Eric patted the war horse. Taking a large breath, he began making camp. "I wonder what is for dinner." Soon he heard the words, "Watch out below." He heard an object fall next to him, and that's when he saw a good-sized fish at his feet, "That is service. Thank you, Gustav and Ariel." He heard the eagle call and heard, "You're welcome. You will need it tomorrow for strength. We need to find our dinner, and tomorrow we will join you at sunrise." He slept with his sword at his side. His sleep was interrupted several times by strange sounds of the forest.

There were strange hoots and animal calls that seemed to lend eeriness to the dark woods. When he had camped with his father, someone always seemed to keep the campfire burning. Now he was alone. "Thank you, Father, for our many adventures that have prepared me for this grand journey." He finally found a comfortable position and slept soundly.

He awoke as the sun was cresting over the distant mountains. He restarted a small fire and warmed himself with a morning brew of certain grains. Finding a large stone to sit on, he looked up the trail. Looking at his mount and patting the sword at his side, he thought, "Will I do any good in this crazy world today?

"Well, I had better get started. I hope you are ready, Gustav. I certainly will need your help." Looking up, he saw the soaring raptor in the cloudless morning sky and heard, "I am glad my love has such a beautiful covering of feathers and I have my fur coat. It is still quite chilly up here, but we are warming with the morning sun."

Together, with Ariel and Gustav above, the young adventurer traversed several areas of cultivated land. "You may see her castle just over the next rise." Ariel, with her white ferret knight, had seen the many small farms that appeared to encircle Elena's castle. Though he knew that she knew, the young fellow cautiously crawled up a small rise. As the afternoon sun warmed all within this valley, he felt chilled as he saw the familiar guards and the hounds of Elena. "How are we to approach, Gustav?" He heard the voice say, "Rest and prepare."

Eric paced and thought of just how to address this challenge. He heard Ariel ask him a question. "What say you, young one?" He looked at his meager supplies and armament, then he commented, "It looks like we should create a grand diversion. This to draw out Elena and her minions. One of us could enter the fortress and free Sir Matthew."

"I volunteer for that part of this escapade. There are some friends within who could help." The boy looked up to the circling duo. "You have friends in this realm? This said by the boy of youth, speaking somewhat incredulously to the sky. "We have friends in high places and cats in low places." He rolled his eyes and moaned. "You don't speak to cats too?" Then he laughed. "What an odd happening we have here. I won't ask anymore, so let us find that distraction."

Gustav from his vantage point noticed a strange sight located at the edge of a tract of land. Ariel flew down to what appeared to be an old carriage. The body of the former transporter had weathered away, but the frame was intact, as were the beautiful wheels. "This must be a relic of times past." This said by the ferret as he crawled around the frame and walked up to the wheels that were still attached. "Let us call Young Eric. I think we have found part of his plan."

CHAPTER TWENTY-ONE
THE PUMPKIN REMEMBERS

The young son, heir to a small realm and just thirteen seasons of age, approached the old carriage frame. "Wow, I think my gallant steed could pull it, but where do I stand?" "Good question, young knight. I think I carry an answer here in my satchel." Eric watched as the ferret planted the orange seed beneath the frame. "Finally, you want my magic. Thank you. I have rested long enough. Here I go."

They all watched as tiny green tentacles emerged from the ground and began climbing the old carriage frame. At the center of the frame, he saw an orb begin to grow. It took his breath away at the awesomeness of this particular magic. He backed away as the pumpkin grew quickly. Though the old frame was fortunately very sturdy, it still creaked and groaned as the weight of the pumpkin increased. "A pumpkin coach, how quaint it appears. There are vines to attach to the horse and squeaky wheels to herald our approach. That, dear Orange, is a splendid diversion." With that said, he noticed something strange appearing on the side of the orb. It was a very animated face. "Hello, Eric."

The boy was struck silent as he stood there in openmouthed astonishment. "I feel very light-headed." He then sat and stared up at the magic. "What say you, high flyers, and young adventurer?" "We are dually impressed with such a feat. Where did you come from, tiny delicious morsel of magic?"

The face appeared with a thoughtful expression. "Whatever happened to my lineage occurred many, many seasons ago. It must have been a marvelous happening, though it may not be a grand as the one from my past. I just know that I can make something happen again." Eric awoke from his stupor and arose. He walked around the strange transport and pulled at the vines attached to it. "How do I look, young knight-driver?" He said nothing and checked the wheels and looked underneath. "I have heard of carriages, but until now I have never seen one, especially one like you. Where do I sit, Orange?"

Orange the pumpkin groaned slightly, and then there appeared a depression located to the front which could be used as a seat. Then steps appeared that went from bottom to the top of the carriage. "Bring up your beautiful animal and see if he will tolerate being attached to me." Patting the horse gently, Eric brought it to the front of the carriage. "This may seem strange to him, so hold him tight while my vines do their work." As the first vine touched him, the great steed reared up in fear. "Be still, my friend, I'll be gentle with you." His old stallion quieted quickly and allowed the vines to caress him and formed a soft halter with lines leading to the orb that could be used to lead and direct him. "Climb aboard, Eric, and take the reins." The boy found the steps and, grabbing hold of a vine, found his seat. He called softly to the old farm horse that began to find new energy. It appeared to stand taller as it sniffed the air, stamping his hooves. The great stallion looked back at Eric, nodding its head.

He took hold of the reins/vines, as they appeared strong to the pull yet soft as they encircled his stallion. "You may say that I am ready. How are you, Ariel and Gustav?" "You need to practice. Try persuading that beautiful animal to pull you around this neighborhood. Ariel and I will approach Elena's place, where I will enter and find my friends. You, young friend, will be needed to create this diversion. Let us say, when the sun begins to set." Feeling the magic around him, he called out, "Sunset seems like a good time to die." The orb contracted and expanded and then spoke. "You will not die on my watch, young man."

The great bird flew on toward Elena's castle. As it was late afternoon, Gustav held to his mate as they circled the fortress. "I believe that I see the window that I first entered." Ariel also saw it, and she gently landed, and the knight dismounted and quickly scampered like a ferret to the safety of the wall. It was a short climb to the open window as he looked within and saw all was clear. "I'll see you soon, love. I'll start looking for the cats. Hopefully they'll remember me."

Ariel said not a word for fear of the hounds hearing her. She rose quickly into the cooling air. Finding a perch on a large dead pine tree that was still standing, she began to preen her golden feathers and watched as the events began. Ariel sighed and, in a great leap, found flight back to find the young driver of the pumpkin.

Within a short time, he was found. The young Eric was quickly learning the nuances of driving the strange pumpkin carriage. "Am I going too fast, Orange?" This said as the orange carriage was careening down a country road. He pulled back on the reins and felt what seemed as a sigh. "Wow, I think we did fine, young man. We will be a great diversion." It startled them both as Ariel landed on the back of the pumpkin. "I need to rest for a moment." Her lovely voice transmitted to the two. "You can alight on the carriage anytime you wish, beautiful raptor of the skies." The great orange carriage could be seen with what appeared to be a very benevolent smile.

"Young Eric, I believe Gustav has had time to reach Matthew within the dungeon." He looked at the beautiful raptor as she carefully walked close to the young man. Reaching out, Eric gently caressed her feathered body and then pulled back. "I am sorry that I didn't ask permission to touch you." He heard her thoughts as a whispered voice was heard, "My dear Eric, it has been a long time since I was touched by a man. Thank you. Oh, to correct myself, I have been cuddled by a very handsome ferret." The three of them giggled for a moment, and then all was silent as the returned to the business at hand.

"You and your orange carriage may head for the castle. When you arrive, you may begin to circle the fortress. This will draw Elena out in the open. Do not let her catch you. I will return to you soon." She extended her great wings and lifted off into the cooling air. "Let us be off, mighty Orange of magic." The stallion was quick to respond as it pulled the carriage onto the rutted country road. "As someone once said, 'We are off,' it should be said, and 'We must be daft, for we are on a fool's venture.'" The boy shook his head in disagreement. "We may be daft, but this is a venture of honor and rescue. I am glad we are here."

CHAPTER TWENTY-TWO

BATTLE ROYALE

"You are correct, young man. I just get caught up in the moment." The great carriage appeared to grimace as the jarring of the road vibrated through its greatly inflated body. The road was difficult to manage, as sometimes they slowed to a crawl to avoid deep ruts. Soon they were on a long stretch of ancient highway that appeared to lead directly to Elena's fortress. It was not hard to miss, as there were many lanterns illuminating the structure.

Upon the walls of the fortress, one of the tall stately guards called an alarm as the strange vehicle was sighted. "What, pray tell, is that?" The female soldier pointed out into the failing light as the carriage was spotted. "Call out to our Mistress Elena." The other guard turned and looked into the stable area. "I believe she knows already." Indeed, Elena knew, and she was assisting with preparing her black carriage. The four beautiful black stallions appeared nervous as they pulled at the harnesses. "Be still, my dears, you will run soon. We will capture the one who dares to challenge me." She called the hounds. They were ready.

Within the walls of her castle, another challenge was being issued. The ferret knight had found the cats, and the gray mousers were now charging through the hallway leading to the main door of the dungeon. The soldier on duty saw the cats approaching and, without thinking, called out, "Halt, who goes there?" Then looking around, she realized the awkwardness of the command. She began walking toward the small gray squad of felines as they appeared not to be listening to her or even to be undaunted by her challenge. Instead, she thought a voice called to her. "Give us the key, and you will not be harmed." Her face registered alarm as she searched for the person giving the command.

Shaking her head, she appeared to be awakening from a stupor. "Why am I here?" She found the only key on her belt. "Why seek you this key?" She searched for the being, but to no avail. A white ferret was noticed on a ledge about her. "Why is there a weasel?" "That is a ferret. Please, just lay it down, and be off with you, back to your family." The soldier complied and ran, screaming.

The soldier's cries echoed thought the hallway as Gustav found the heavy key. He looked at the cats, and they eyed him. Now they all lay in a protective circle in front of the great door, purring and grooming. The ferret found claw holds and began to climb toward the barred window. "This is hard work, Elizabeth. What do I do when I get there?" "You find a narrow ledge that leads to the window. When you get there, drop the key inside and call out the prisoner." Gustav found it and carefully skirted across the ledge to the window. "I am so tired, Elizabeth. My tiny strength is waning." It felt as hands to his back as he reached the window. The key was held by one of his claws and now felt as a feather. He pushed it through, and it clanked on the stone floor.

A bearded fellow approached hesitantly to the key. He was unkempt, dirty, and the key was eyed with suspicion. "Why is there a key on my floor?" He reached down and picked it up. His face appeared to brighten the more he felt and caressed the metal. He looked at the great door and then to the key. It was, as one would call, a candle suddenly illuminating a darkened hall.

Laughing now, he felt for the keyhole and found it. Inserting it and turning slowly, he heard a click. "What do we have here?" He found a small handle and pulled. The creaking door could be heard throughout the castle, but no one hearkened to it. All were focused on what was happening outside the walls, as a strange orange transport was circling the walls. No orders for defense had been given, but several archers could be seen notching their arrows. They heard a screaming command from the Mistress Elena. "No one will harm it, except me." The large doors of the outer walls were opened, and the Lady Elena exited, riding atop the great carriage and wielding the long whip that snapped with a bang. Her long red curls reaching out behind her as magical flames.

The stallions felt the snap of the whip. There was no pain, just a desire to run. She caught sight of Eric's carriage, and off they went in pursuit. Elena began firing strange rockets that appeared to be aimed at the fleeing vehicle. "I think we have her attention." As one of the rockets burst just above them, the pumpkin winced and, frowning, commented, "Stay on the task, young man." All within the tiny realm watched the fireworks and wondered. The great eagle saw all of this in the distance and found her goal. She circled the smaller castle, a neighbor of Elena and concerned parents of Eric. Ariel perched on a nearby wall and found the parents. Stephen had seen the pyrotechnic display and ordered his horse brought to the gate. "I must travel quickly to Eric. I could have sworn that I heard a voice told me to hurry." Constance looked at her husband quizzically and smiled. "Be off with you, my love. Be safe, and look after the heir to the throne."

The gates opened, and the worried father charged into the evening air. He knew the roads and the countryside. The open land and hills beckoned to him as he chose to go cross-country. The mighty horse that he rode was a lighter mount than most. Stephen had ventured onto open fields with this well-muscled beauty in happier times. She was a mare bred for speed. He trusted her and spoke quiet, reassuring words as he led the charger toward the hills surrounding Elena's fortress. "I hope Eric is okay." Again he heard the voice. "He is doing fine. Just be careful, father of a future knight." In all the rush, the gallant, caring father looked around and about to locate the voice. All he saw was a large raptor that appeared to be following him. "I hope that is my good luck charm." He stopped at the crest of a hill overlooking what appeared to be a carriage wreck.

Young Eric was feeling the thrill of the chase. The old horse that had been pulling the orange carriage had now found new vigor. The only arrow that had been fired at him had barely missed him and was embedded in the hide of the pumpkin. "I certainly hope that does not hurt. I'll pull it out if you wish." He heard a brief laugh. "I felt nothing, but thanks for your concern. We must continue to lead this fair damsel, or shall I say, fair witch on this wild chase so as to tire her. The longer we go, the more we will have a chance of changing the spell that has engulfed the small realm."

It was a wild scene as one could see the horse-drawn pumpkin carriage pursued by a pack of hounds, mounted warriors, and the black carriage pulled by those magnificent stallions. It seemed that Elena had taken no notice of the fact that she had been circling her castle. It was almost comical to those left standing on the fortress walls as they watched their mistress and her entourage continue to pass by the front gate. One of those atop the wall looked to the other and asked, "Why in heaven's name are we standing here watching this parade?"

Her partner was looking around at the castle at the grand parade below and then, shaking her head, said, "You know, I really want to go home." They both found the stairs and joined others as they found the open front gate. Elena glanced back at her castle and the open gate; she then noticed the crowd that had gathered there and were appearing to cheer as she passed. She absentmindedly waved back and then returned to a concentration on the chase.

Young Eric also saw this cheering crowd and thinking out loud, thought, "What a very strange evening this has become." He then heard the voice of Ariel. "You are doing very well. Just be careful as you round those turns." Just as those words were spoken, he heard the pumpkin speak. "We have a problem. Please hold on." The pumpkin carriage was beginning to swerve as one of the old wheels began to pull off the axle. The great horse that had been pulling this contrivance lurched ahead as he broke free from its harness.

The carriage made sharp turn and began to roll as Eric jumped off. Behind him, Elena pulled the reins so as to miss the wreck, and her carriage also began to roll. As the dust settled, one can see the great pumpkin mash with an old horse nibbling at the remains. It was as though the spell had been broken, for the guards were now quietly dismounting and looking for their mistress. The hounds too quieted and walked carefully up to their mistress and sat in a circle, with one of them walking up to her and licking her face. From out the castle gate strode a somewhat bedraggled but focused companion of Elena. The hounds made way for him as he found his love and knelt to her side. He carefully picked her up in his arms and began to carry her back to the castle.

CHAPTER TWENTY-THREE

RECONCILIATION

As though coming out of a stupor, she looked up into his face and rested her head on his chest. "I'm so sorry about all this spell business." As he was walking toward the castle gate, he noticed a rider approaching. He saw that it was his neighbor, Stephen. The rider said nothing as he galloped by and quickly dismounted. He began looking for son and saw him in a distance. The young man was lying facedown in the soft earth and was not moving. "Eric!" he cried as he ran to his first and only son. He knelt by his side and carefully touched him. He brushed back the hair from his face and then gently shook him. He watched and was gratified as his son awakened. The lad slowly rolled over and, with the help of his father, sat up and began to look around. "What a fine mess we have made. Is she going to be okay, Father?"

His father looked at him and smiled. "I believe that we will all be fine, my son, great thanks to you and those who have helped." It appeared that Matthew and his lady had begun to reenter the castle. Matthew turned and looked at the messy end and then looked at the father and son. He waved to them. "We'll meet soon with you and all of our neighbors to make amends." Stephen waved back and nodded, and then he and his son watched as the hounds also appeared to be reentering. No longer were they snarling howling beasts but appeared to be playing among themselves, as dogs sometimes do. The mounted warriors also were reentering, but they were walking and leading their horses. Some were quiet, as others were talking back and forth as neighbors who had just met. This terrible spell had been broken. As the great doors of the fortress were closing, a massive pyrotechnic display could be seen illuminating the castle and the countryside. All would be well.

All within this realm were awakened, and some knew that change was near. As all were beginning to celebrate, no one noticed a white ferret searching among the orange debris. "Well, my pumpkin friend, here is another nice mess we've made." A small, weak voice was heard, "What a very wild ride that was." Gustav quickly grabbed a seed and placed it in the well-worn satchel and ran to find his partner. "I am ready if you are, grand golden raptor."

The scream of the great bird could be heard as he held up his claws in greeting. With a flutter of her great wings, she landed next to him. "It is nice to land, and now, my gentle knight, you may find your perch." As she nudged him with her beak, he caressed her. "What a day. Thank you, Elizabeth. This has been a challenging travel." "You, my two loves, deserve all the credit. Elena and Matthew have been reunited, Eric and his father have grown together, and two small realms will be the better. Rest for a few days, and then you must travel to the north." In unison, she heard, "North, why must we go?" There was that sweet giggle of their dear friend. "I am sorry, but there is a great need for your presence." Gustav sighed, then he called to his mate, "Let's you and I go fishing tomorrow." As the lifted off, he heard, "Marvelous idea, my dear knight."

CHAPTER TWENTY-FOUR

THE SCAVENGER

After resting near the castle of Stephen, the trio felt the call to the north. After traveling for many weeks, one day they were flying high above a wide and deep canyon. They noticed a deathly quiet, as there were no signs of life below as they entered a large open plain. The view from above was shocking, as it appeared that the valley had been the scene of a battle of great losses. Spiraling down from windy heights, the trio observed the great carnage. Below them, they could see the various flights of carrion eaters. The great birds were all were part of an unorganized band of scavengers cleaning up after another bloody skirmish of history that would never be noted in the books of man.

The days had passed since the battle had been won and lost. The land was soaked with the blood of the fallen. Surrounding the fallen, the trio could see the dark wings of the next act in this play of life. Many vultures were leaving as many were just beginning the feast. "I've never seen such a theater of the macabre," said the ferret knight as he clung to his love.

She circled and dived above the scene. They could see the various combatants, as many lay looking up to their final view of life. The winds of that day were as great sighs of mourning as they caressed the battle flags that fluttered silently. Some thought that the winds of battle carried the souls of the vanquished to rest. As Ariel, Gustav, and Orange viewed the great plains, the clamor of metallic sounds could be heard. "Do you see that person?" This asked by the raptor.

A lone soldier appeared to be walking through the great fields. "Could this be the living trying to help those wounded rejoin their comrades in battle?" This was asked by the magical seed. As the soldier walked, they could see that he was carrying scavenged wares. This individual clanked and rattled noisily as he appeared to be seeking shields, swords, and breastplates. They can see his sunburned face, and his clothing appeared ragged and his feet were covered with strips of leather. Through this walking tower of scrap, they noticed that it was a woman. She appeared old, one step from death. If you looked in her eyes, you would see that her eye movements were quick—she was a survivor. The warring armies often returned to claim the spoils for themselves, and they did not appreciate the work of independent scavengers who pick the bones like the dark-winged carrion birds.

As they continued observing, they saw that she had reached the body of the tall figure in gentle repose. The warrior wore armor with hooded helmet and visor to shield his identity. The helmet was a beautiful work of metal sculpture. They heard her shout, "It's mine." She then kicked the warrior to assess life. No life was noted. Then she moved to the head of the warrior and began to pull off the great helmet. With difficulty, this armored sculpture began to slip off the head of the warrior. The helmet released its grip of the dead soldier. The scavenger was holding onto the prize with both hands, and with its release, she fell backward onto the loose soil.

Laughing loudly, she held the sculpture aloft and began to examine it. Holding up the helmet, she noted the blue sky and the various flying birds in the background. She then looked closely at the face on the helmet. She wiped the dust from her leathered face and looked closely at the helmet. "What is this," she said with a sense of urgency. She struggled to her feet and examined the body more closely. Liberal amounts of dirt and grime hid the face of the soldier. The old one whispered softly, "Who are you to wear such a work of art?" She began to absentmindedly rub off the dirt that covered him and then wiped more in earnest. "No . . . It can't be."

CHAPTER TWENTY-FIVE

A KNIGHT ARISES

She then gently moved the head and saw a single braid of hair at the back of her head. A low moan issued from the body, and the ancient one, eyes wide with fright, promptly fell faint on the field of battle. The woman warrior arose with difficulty and finally stood. She continued to stagger as she tried to awaken. She looked around at the scene and then at her feet where lay the scavenger. "Maybe I should just put you out of your misery, you follower of the carrion eaters."

The warrior found her sword and pulled it out of its scabbard. With a two-handed grip, she raised the weapon over her head. She then drove the blade into the soft earth next to the old one. She looked down at the female beneath her and appeared to ponder as to what she will do next. She reconsidered any final action for the moment. Kneeling, she tried to awaken the old woman. After slapping her face a few times rather briskly, the scavenger began to moan. She was now moaning and crawling around the ground. "Maybe I should just put you out of your misery."

The gray-haired woman finally came to her senses and uttered a plea. "Oh, great maiden, sister of battle, forgive me for disturbing your death sleep. I am a scavenger, and I survive on scraps of war." The warrior looked at the scavenger of the field and then they both looked down at the helmet that the hag was still clutching close to her body. "My head aches from the manner of relieving me of that scrap metal, woman." "I am sorry, warrior. My assessment was wrong, and you most certainly are alive." Gingerly touching her ribs, she said, "Your manner of assessment reflects the attitude of this great field of bleaching bones: contact." The woman carefully walked up to the warrior and offered to wrap her chest with strips of cloth to ease the pain. Though confused with this offer, she allowed the hag to wrap her chest, and indeed, it did appear to relieve the pain.

The old woman spoke again. "These fortunes of war are how we survive and how I provide for my husband and myself. My husband is a fallen warrior. He was robbed of his dignity and his legs. I found him, and I dragged him back to shelter. I stopped the weeping of his wounds, fed him, and saved him from the mourning winds. We live at a humble farm within the hills. This where we care for each other. It is at our home and our small kingdom." The warrior looked at the woman and then into her soul. She saw such depth, such sweetness, and all tempered by survival. "Woman," said she. "My name is Gretchen, and I have been a warrior until this day." Their conversation was interrupted by the scream of the large golden eagle flying above them. Little did they know that the ferret knight and his love have seen an old friend.

As Gustav held on tightly to the small rope that bound him to his feathered love and together they rejoiced, they swooped above the scavenger and the warrior. "Do you think they wonder why this great bird is swooping at them?" This asked by Gustav as he hung precariously to his love as she dove and did great loops of celebration. Another voice was heard as Orange spoke. "Hey you two, I'm getting really dizzy, and that's really hard for a pumpkin seed to do." The trio tired quickly of the celebration and followed the two beneath them.

"My name is Mary," said the gray-haired lady of the plains. She offered help for the warrior's comfort. "I have herbs and potions to help you heal, and I will share my small portion of air-dried fruit and vegetables. We must leave now before the enemy returns." Still wincing from the sharp pains in her ribs and weak from blood loss, Gretchen helped Mary carry the armor from the field. Gretchen thought quietly to herself, *From captain of a small militia to soldier of fortune and finally a scavenger of scraps with a strange old hag. How strange, this life.*

The two women contrasted as they walked slowly toward the rolling hills surrounding the plain. Mary touched the shoulder of the soldier gingerly and then pointed toward a tall hill. "We live in a small hidden valley just on the other side of that hill. We have a thatched-roof house we built under a small group of trees. Our family consists of two cows, chickens, and numerous other animals in our small Eden." As they slowly walked toward the hill, they had to stop to get a better grip on all the bounty.

CHAPTER TWENTY-SIX

MY WOUNDED WARRIOR

Gretchen was beginning to relax and heal slowly as she looked across the plains. "Old one, as I see all of this that surrounds us, I consider my awakening. I wondered as to whether I wished to be awakened. Now I'm here and alive. There must be a reason why we have met. I am fortunate to be working with you. I owe you service for a time, in reward of your saving ways."

"Sister and veteran of wars, you owe me nothing." Aside from my mate, there are few people who traveled through this land that I seek to converse with or meet. We only meet occasionally with peddlers, who will sometimes purchase metal. First, you must eat, heal, and, of course, rest. That is, after you have words with a cackling hen." Gretchen stopped and then looked at the hag. "You have a cackling hen? Do not all farms have such an animal?" The older lady laughed, almost cackling, as she answered, "Ah, yes, that name does bring to mind strange thoughts. Alan and I have little names for each other. I'm what he calls the hissing goose, yet I have no idea what he calls me such a title. On the other hand, you will understand his name."

After walking through very small and narrow canyons, they came to the end of what appeared to be a box canyon. Walking to the wall, they turned, and that was when she noticed an entrance. Upon going through a narrow opening, they entered a large and fertile valley with a stand of trees to one side. Looking closely, Gretchen could see a small farm hidden beneath the trees. The closer they walked to the small grove of trees, she could see a thatched-roof house and a couple of shelters for animals.

"Old man," the woman cried, "I come with a friend." Gretchen heard a brief noise, and then all was quiet except the animals. Mary quietly stepped back, folded her arms, and, with a wicked grin, watched the play begin. Gretchen slowly pulled out her sword and, turning toward the noise, said, "Give me a sign, man, as to where you sit. I will come quickly and lay this armored bounty upon you. This may give you rest from you worries, cackling hen indeed."

The voice appeared harsh and almost a loud whisper. "Hissing goose, where did you find this wench with her tartness and maybe strength of the warrior? I need not this gift of a second woman. Feed her, let her wash and rest. Then send her on her way." Mary was laughing so hard that she fell back on her bottom. Gretchen looked at Mary, then at the noise from behind the barn.

Mary called out again. "Please stop with your dialogue. I have awakened this warrior from her death sleep." "Have you told your armored friend why you're called hissing goose? He then continued, "I will tell her. You are named for your defensive ways of furious flapping of your wings and honking words of harassment, all in the same breath. Now I have two of you. Be gone! I stand corrected. You, warrior, are welcome to stay for a short while. You may take the hissing goose and, with her, seek the plains and leave me with the chickens. Those feathered beasts appreciate me when I feed them. Be off with you now and give me rest, or reap the anger of the wheeled knight."

Gretchen became curious of the voice of this so-called wheeled knight. She cautiously approached the small barn. Then, using great stealth, she carefully walked around the small enclosure. Then she heard him. "Come on out, warrior, and meet a fellow survivor. I have your fate in my sights. Walk forward, no sudden moves, and meet me." As she came around, she found a man sitting in a strange chair. He was holding a crossbow at the ready. Gretchen, having experienced enough war, placed her sword back in its scabbard. Then said the tall female warrior, "How quick you defend, wheeled knight. Your hissing goose has brought you a great wealth of armor and strange mobility. I yield and offer my humble services to you and Mary." She then knelt, waited, and listened.

This warrior in his wheeled chair pushed himself to a spot in front of Gretchen. Touching her head gently, he asked, "A warrior with honor, will you please rise and push my chair toward our home? Join us to supper and drink sweet nectar. Mary, let us dine with this traveler. Give food to this royalty."

"Indeed, the meat is cooked, and the fruit was freshly picked. The nectar will taste cool and sweet. Come to the table, and let us dine under the shade of the tree that also shelters the grave of our first and only child." Alan looked up at Gretchen. "We lost the child at birth. She was beautiful, and we miss her." As Gretchen began to push Alan's chair, he began to roll himself turning the large wheels with his strong callused hands. The chair he rolled appeared quite remarkable. It was a strongly built chair mounted upon an axle that held two rounded shields. The edges of the shields were hand formed so as to be gripped. She saw the yard and was impressed. It was swept clear of obstacles and allowed for great mobility by the wheeled knight. She marveled at this knight as he rolled about with a short sword at the ready and a crossbow, also ready with a quiver of bolts. Though his legs were motionless, his muscled shoulders and arms pushed it well over the uneven ground. There were cleared pathways throughout their domain. Though it was slightly hilly, they remained free from debris.

They sat under the shade of a large tree and talked. Mary scurried about, bringing platters of smoked meats and sweet fruits. As they sat upon the crude wooden chairs, Alan looked lovingly at his bustling mate and then looked at Gretchen. He pointed briefly at the gray-haired woman who no longer looked like a hag. Though her face was sunburned and tanned from hours on the plains, she had piercing blue eyes and now she was showing a sweet smile. He whispered to Gretchen, "I call her my hissing goose with great love in my heart. She is my soul and benefactress. Yes, her hair does appear as a swarming nest of bees, and her hands are callused and worn like mine, yet she is the love of my life. If she had not found me, I could have been brought and left in a village or township. I could have become a beggar in the streets to live a very short life. Instead, I have purpose as I work alongside this great hissing goose. She works from sunrise to late evening. With all this great wealth, she is my sweet Mary. I am called Alan of the Seven-Year War. Thanks to her, I am a cackling hen and alive. Young warrior, please stay with us for a season. My mate and I could use an extra pair of strong hands. Your sweet smile could counter the sounds of a cackling hen and a hissing goose."

Mary shouted, "That invitation comes from me too, my dear. Please stay a while, repair and replenish yourself."

Gretchen waved to them both, and she walked away to find some privacy. She sat gazing around their small kingdom. She heard all the chickens and cows and various other small animals, including an old horse they used for plowing. She then heard an old familiar voice. "You are looking well, dear friend." With excitement in her voice and looking around frantically, she said, "Oh, my gracious," with tears streaming from her eyes. Then she heard the duo say, "Hello, Gretchen." She was frantic now; she barely noticed the eagle perched high above her.

The old defender of the realm and his hissing goose watched the strange animated conversation the young female knight was having with an unknown being. She appeared to be crying and then laughing as she walked down the well-worn pathways. Suddenly, she stopped and looked back at her two benefactors. She motioned to them and mouthed the words: "We'll talk about this."

"Maybe it's the stress of the battle she just survived, or maybe it's the heat." He continued to whisper to his mate, "Let's just sit back, relax, and wait for her explanation." The two of them turned their backs to her to give her privacy. Occasionally, one or the other will give a quick glance to see how the warrior was doing. Finally, the young knight began to walk back to the couple. "You probably think I'm going a bit batty, don't you?" They both slowly shook their heads and said, "No, we thought it might be the sun or maybe surviving the battle." Gretchen just laughed and then motioned for them to have a seat under the shade of the tree.

"It seems so long ago that I was a king's guard in our realm located far over the mountains. The knight whose position I took was spelled by an evil witch. But the evil witch also laid a trap for this brave knight. The trap was so evil." She paused and then, with tears coursing down her face and with a catch in her voice, continued, "Anyone touching the spelled knight was also spelled.

"His love was the one spelled as a predator, whose first goal was to kill the king's guard, her sweet love. Fortunately, the predator's desires were abated by the spell of a good witch. There always seems to be a catch in these situations. The original spell could not be changed, and so here they remain as creatures of nature. Fate was with them as they were given quests by the good witch, or as she is now called, the Good Fairy. They receive calls to those in need.

"Somehow, they have find ways to change lives. In their quest, they found me and watched as I rose from the dead. What joy it is to hear the voices of those from the past and to meet new friends such as you." The old couple of the plains looked at this brave warrior and saw her joy in reunion. "We are so happy to have found you and to witness this grand reunion. Who are these creatures, and can we hear them?" "I believe that is up to them to reveal themselves. If they choose, they will speak to me, and I'll let you know of their thoughts. Gustav just commented to me that he wished know more of your history. He fears hearing voices will cause others to think less of you."

The old woman, survivor of the plains, began laughing so hard that she was rolling up on the ground with gales of laughter. The wheeled knight was also laughing hysterically. With tears in his eyes, he looked up to the warrior princess, saying, "Let them speak, for we always hear voices. We hear the voices of those who have passed on from the fields of battle. We find them and mourn. These fallen speak to us every time we are on the plains of battle. My comrades in battle, who have left this grand earth, also speak to me often."

"Thank you for your service, wheeled knight. We seek not to disturb your life and thank you for this time to reunite with a fellow member of our realm." They heard this voice in unison and slowly looked around for the source. They hugged each other and then, looking up at the young maiden, commented, "Your voices are as if you were standing next to us. Are you near?" "Think of us as beings moving through the skies, much like that golden eagle you may see you over there high above you." This said by the ferret knight as he looked down upon the scene below.

It was a strange reunion as Gretchen recounted her decision to leave the realm of King Angus. She joined as a man and kept her identity secret. Not one warrior challenged her, for she was a formidable opponent. During the first brief conflicts that were encountered, she marveled at the bravery of those around her. Her final day of combat found their forces greatly outnumbered. She sought from her leader permission to regroup and return to battle when their forces regrouped.

Her leader would not be led by such a new upstart. He sent them all to their final battle. Greatly outnumbered, with her foe bent on their destruction, she was knocked to the ground by the glancing blow from an ax. The enemy was ferocious in their attack and looked to each of the dead and dying as an individual victory. Their cries of triumph were accentuated by the smashing sound of the ax as a coup de grace to the wounded. Somehow, she was overlooked in all the mayhem.

Her mate, Karl, was seen in a dream. He called to her to come join in joyous reunion. Then slowly, as if rising with the wind, she could see his field of battle. "Come to me," he cried out, and with a final wave, the dream faded. She knew that he too had joined the mourning winds. She spoke of their first meeting. He was the only one to have known her true identity before the first battle. None of her squad members had questioned her prowess or fierceness in combat. Then this mercenary appeared.

CHAPTER TWENTY-SEVEN

LOVE SO BRIEF

He joined the ranks of warriors who had been together from the beginning. Behind his back, the others referred to him as one who fought for the highest bidder. All learned quickly of his abilities as they watched him in mock combat. No one spoke again of his price or his dark, seeking eyes. Gretchen avoided him at all cost. She knew that somehow, he would see through her charade.

It happened late one evening. She had bumped into him as they were finishing the evening meal. She quickly walked away, but not before he called out to her, "You." She stopped, facing away from him. He walked up to her and appeared very curious. She always wore her helmet for concealment, but tonight her visor was up in the subdued light. Her skin was darkened to break up her features. "Who are you?" he asked as he went nose to nose with her. "Argo of the Angus Realm," she countered.

He then whispered to her, "I am your protector, Young Argo." She took a deep breath and stated, "I need no protection from the likes of you." He laughed and looked around, noticing that no one was close to them as he spoke. "Ah, my seasoned warrior with dainty lips and unblemished skin." He stopped abruptly as he felt a dagger's tip at his chest.

He held up his hands and shrugged. "I have been embarrassingly wrong before." She whispered a response, "I would think with your weak eyes and twisted mind that you would have learned a lesson by now." He walked away and into the darkness. In the early morning, she was carefully attending to her bodily needs, a noise was heard. Quickly arranging herself, she sought out the source of noise, moving with stealth, and with sword unsheathed, she moved. The warrior Karl came from behind a nearby tree. With a stern look and slight smile, he spoke to her. "I seek not a young man with feminine face, but I seek the hidden beauty behind your battle mask. You are that beauty that I have watched since I first arrived."

"It must be your dreams that muddle your poor mind," she taunted him. "Before we depart from our training, you must sing to me, fair maiden warrior." She took his arm, and together they walked a good distance away from the others. Taking off her helmet, she looked at him and smiled. "I will sing songs of remembrance and love." He held her in his arms in a secluded grove as his dark eyes looked through the mists of memories, of loves lost and found. Later, before they were to meet the great foe, she and Karl returned to King Angus for a last reunion. The tears were flowing freely from all as she recounted this brief history. She excused herself from this dialogue and looked for a place to rest.

The warrior found fresh hay on which to sleep. She too had many thoughts and questions of life. It was hard to find sleep as she meditated upon this reunion of such joy. The glowing embers of the setting sun warmed her and helped her sleep. She also dreamed of her love as he lay on the dry, sandy soil, breathing his last. She knelt and kissed his brow, then his lips. With tears flowing freely, she whispered, "Dear soul, remember the grove and our song."

He appeared to nod and began humming a beautiful art song. He coughed and began to hum again, and the sound became a breeze that caressed and comforted her. She awoke later with a start as she orientated herself to the strangeness of the location. Then she said she drank some sweet nectar and dozed.

Gretchen slept and dreamed of families, loves, and the sweetness of peace. Early the next morning, she awoke and looked out upon the mists as they hovered close to the ground. She felt strangeness and then heard a sound. It was as if something were crawling toward her. Was it a beast of the night seeking her out? She reached for his sword and realized she'd left it on the log. She did have a short dagger that she always had in her boot. She prepared for the attack.

Through the haze, she could make out the barn doors slowly opening and watched a shadowy thing approaching. It was crawling across the dirt floor. Then she recognized the man as he called out to her. "It is my Mary. She left early for the plains and has not returned."

CHAPTER TWENTY-EIGHT

HE IS MY MATE, IT IS MY CHAIR, AND THIS IS MY CROSSBOW

The pink horizon of the breaking dawn silhouetted the wheeled knight and the warrior. As they left the neatly swept trails of the farm, they encountered more hazards for the wheeled warrior. Soon, Alan looked back to Gretchen. "Mary would often push me until the plains become less littered with rocks. These flat lands can sometimes be very smooth, as they are constantly brushed by the winds." They found a place of concealment in a large stand of high bushes.

They have stopped and began listening to the sounds of the early morning. The wind was gentle as they saw a large bird of prey overhead. They searched the land. There were many sounds, some even seemed as voices. As they scanned the area, he whispered, "Do not be deceived. In the early light, there are many scattered illusions. It's hard to separate the real from the imagined. Look, listen, and then focus. I know she is there, for I can feel her presence."

High above in the cool morning air flew the great raptor and her companion. They too are watching and searching, for they have heard the conversation between Alan and Gretchen. "I'm afraid for her safety," said the ferret. The great bird spoke in hushed tones of thought to her rider. "I believe that I see her, but we should not alarm those two on the ground." They continued to circle and wait.

Gretchen gave the universal sign of silence with a raised forefinger to the lips and then signed to Alan that there were more than five people ahead of them in the distance. "Do you see that lone tree on that small knoll?" "Yes. Is it important?" "That is there where Mary will often go to hide her stashes of metal. Listen for her signal: two long hoots of a bird and one short."

Travel was very slow for the wheeled knight. He did not want to create any noise, so they moved cautiously. Powering the wooden chair over the rough terrain was physically taxing, even for his strong arms. Gretchen tried pushing but found that simply removing obstacles in his way assisted him more than the push. The slowly rising sun began to illuminate all around them as they moved forward. They stopped when they heard the two hoots, followed by a third. "I can move quicker and quieter. Please stay hidden, Alan, while I search and find Mary."

Moving with stealth, Gretchen continued her search for the old woman. She arrived close to the knoll and crept around it, searching for possible hiding places. She became attuned to the sounds of movement; she heard a movement and whirled in a defense with her sword drawn. The old one was crouched behind her with a crossbow lowered, and her right hand was raised in a sign of greeting. "Your mate was worried, woman. Let us leave the bounty and return before that small party of warriors hears us."

The old one nodded her head in agreement and then looked behind Gretchen. Suddenly her tanned, creased, leather face registered fear. She quickly squatted down and called for silence. Gretchen knelt also and slowly turned to see what had startled Mary. Off in the distance, through the morning haze, rode the party that they had heard. They were slowly approaching Alan. They appeared as wild men. Most of the heads were shaved; some who appeared as leaders wore leather helmets. They were all armed with spears, some with scimitars, and others with bows and arrows.

All had seen Alan and, as they approached on their ponies, shouted in recognition of their prey and charged at him. It was too late to call out to Alan, but the hissing goose rose and began to run toward her man. Gretchen grabbed her and held her, covering her mouth with her hand as they both stared in disbelief as Alan was surrounded.

He did not give up, as he pulled on the wheels of his chair as fast as he could. The horseman stopped and remained still for a time and watched the old man. Then they looked at each other, and they looked at the tallest of group. He raised his right arm and let out a very loud cry that echoed over the plain and into the low rolling hills. The sound gradually blended with the cries of the others.

Alan finally stopped his effort to roll away. His wheels were mired in the soft sand, so with grunts and tremendous effort, he turned about to face his antagonists. He was prepared for battle. Mary pulled Gretchen's hand off her mouth and whispered to her, "I should be there with my love to finish those devils on horseback." Gretchen held her and felt her sobs. "I know, my old sister, we must wait for the outcome. Watch them, for it has begun."

CHAPTER TWENTY-NINE

THE WHEELED KNIGHT IN BATTLE

After a few moments of the warriors' cry, the riders pulled away as if in retreat. They rode side by side for a short distance and then slowly turned to face the old warrior. They began in a slow trot, and then in synchronous gallop, they charged. They barely missed him, as one of the riders reached down and touched the top of his head. He inflicted no damage as he raised his fist in triumph. They turned about quickly and began the attack anew. This time with ponies almost shoulder to shoulder, they approached at full gallop. Matthew brought his crossbow to the ready and waited till they were near and then shot a bolt from his crossbow.

One of the riders was hit in the shoulder, and as if in grand choreography, this group of horsemen split to both sides of the knight. As they rode by, their faces registered rage. There were many lengths away from the knight as they pulled up to a dusty stop. Slowly they turned and, with a slow trot, began their final attack. He faced them with arms outstretched in a greeting of warrior to warrior. They didn't play with him this time as they rode by; one of them reached down with a war hammer and, with the blunt side of the weapon, knocked him to the ground. There he lay still on the grassy plain.

As he lay there, all of the mounted warriors heard the scream of an eagle far above. In the distance, they also heard the cry of the female who had lost her mate. The mounted warriors looked around this scene and looked at the clouds above. It was a strange morning as the mourning winds began their cry. They all looked down at the lone man who had shown such spirit. As Alan lay next to the wheeled chair, he moaned and then rolled over on his back, facing the wild men. He called out to them, "Well, my fellow brave warriors, are you going to look at me or finish me off?" One of them faced him, dismounted, and knelt next to him.

This leader of the small group was breathing heavy, and his chest heaved with the effort. He finally took a slow deep breath, relaxed, and then looked at Alan sternly. He was the tallest of the group; his upper body glistened with sweat, and upon his chest were many markings. His skull was devoid of hair. Dark brown eyes were penetrating and were accentuated by his high cheekbones.

His breath was hot and sour. He cocked his head to one side and, with a wide, uncaring grin spoke to Alan, saying, "We will give you time for that, crazy man, but for now we will return to my village and show you to my people."

One of the warriors tied the chair on his horse, and Alan was thrown on top of another horse like a bag of seed and then secured with ropes. The lone knight looked toward the hills and valleys where his love was hidden. Then he shouted, "Don't follow me, go away." Warriors looked at him and just laughed. Within moments, they again heard the scream of an eagle and the cry of a wolf. He knew that, as usual, the hag would not listen. He would be followed, and they would die together, as it should be.

"Do you think he heard?" "He has a hearing of an owl who can hear a mouse eating in its den. Let us prepare to rescue a fellow warrior," said she. They watched as the horseman rode into the distance with their strange trophy. Gretchen watched at the strange procession and spoke. "I should hunt for him alone." Then the lady of the plains reached into her satchel and pulled out a handmade helmet of leather that had small deer horns attached. She then placed it on her head, and the old scavenger of the plains pulled out her crossbow and loaded it. With the strangest grin and tears pouring from of her eyes, she turned her weathered face to the warrior. "He is my mate, it is my chair, and this is my crossbow. You and I will travel together."

She then motioned to a distant tree and fired the crossbow. It found the knot dead-on. "You and I will find him, and we will bring them home." The young woman turned and looked at the target with the bolt. She smiled and put her right hand on her shoulder. "We will do whatever we can to avoid having to respond that way. Let us return to your home quickly and prepare for the chase."

CHAPTER THIRTY

A NAME HONORED

The mounted one was also breathing heavily and sweating profusely as he began to speak. "Why didn't you stay home with your woman? I wonder at your strength and the ability to push that strange chair around the plains." "I was looking for my woman, as you and your warriors interrupted my journey." The warrior bent over and faced him with a snarl, "You shot my brother, legless one." "Your brother still rides doesn't he? I was defending myself, and fortunately for your kin, if it wasn't such a bad shot, he would be resting with your gods." The horseman looked down at Alan and, with a sneer in his voice, said, "The roar of a warrior, the body of a snake, and the brains of an ant. You, walking with this strange chair, tried to defend yourself against mounted warriors?"

"I did, and I will again if given the chance. I am a warrior." He shouted this for all to hear, and then he fainted. They stopped and removed him from the horse. Then they removed the chair. Several of the men picked him up and placed him in the chair. They stood around him and waited for him to awaken. They spoke in quiet whispers as they looked upon this warrior.

Alan awoke in the evening hours. He kept his eyes shut and smelled smoke from a campfire and then slowly opened them and looked at the young warriors. Their leader noticed that he was awake and walked up to him and introduced himself, "I am Karl, the leader of this small group. We are members of a much-larger and formidable army."

Alan looked up to the bronze warrior standing before him. Again he saw that this man was dressed in the skins of animals and then noticed that he wore a leather vest protecting his chest. "Karl? That does not fit such a warrior of the plains." "My name was taken from a white-haired, light-skinned man who almost defeated me in battle. In our final moment of combat, he delayed for a moment of life, and I didn't. I dismounted and approached him and there I realized that this were his last breaths of life.

"He told me his name and called me 'the brave one with no fear.' I was also told of the manner he wished to return to the other side. We honored his request. We placed him on a stand that faced the setting sun. There he was seated in his battle dress, as he said, at the top of the small tower. His soul had left his body, and the structure was set on fire. We moved away from the pyre and watched the billowing smoke rise as though an offering to his god. As it became totally engulfed, we noticed a storm moving toward us. There was thunder and lightning flashing as a rain squall approached through billowing gray clouds.

"We sat on a small knoll a short distance away after we had tethered our horses and covered ourselves with the blankets. We were quiet as this tumult finally extinguished the fire. We felt that this must be a greeter of souls. After we were washed clean and recovered from this great event, I took the name Karl, as this was a good omen. The name will be passed to my son and to his son."

After recounting this story and experience, the warrior spoke. "You will be carried in your wheeled chair to my village. We are building a sled to take you both." The sled was horse-drawn, and the chair was checked into it with Alan facing the rear. He was now able to breathe, see, and think good thoughts. "Be careful, my sweet survivor of the plains." He then saw the golden eagle again perched a short distance away on the limb of the tree. Then he saw what appeared to be small white weasel. The animal was looking at him and then appeared to be waving at him. He then thought to himself, *I must be becoming as daft as my love.* Then he heard in his thoughts a strange voice. "We're here to help you, Alan."

As the horsemen began to prepare to leave, they noticed the wheeled knight, as he appeared to be talking to himself. They looked at each other, shaking their heads. One touched his head and looked at the rest of his companions, then they all agreed that the old man was touched in his head. The man seated in the chair looked around at his kidnappers and continued thinking and conversing through thought. "How, through all that is holy, can an eagle and weasel save me?" Then in the first time since his kidnapping, the survivor began laughing and, with tears in his eyes, slapped his legs and hollered out for all to hear, "I'll be ready."

Right after he had hollered his greeting, he had noticed that the eagle had left and the weasel was gone. Then he looked closely at the eagle and noticed a white patch on the back of the great bird. The white patch appeared to sit up, with one claw holding onto a tiny rope and with the other appearing to wave as they flew away.

As Alan's sharp eyes watched the duo leave, he said to himself, "Ghosts, goblins, and dark riders of the night are meant to the tales of the fireplace. This white weasel is being carried by his mortal enemy on its back." Then he heard the voice again. "I don't mean to correct you, Alan, but I am not a weasel. I am a ferret and a distant relative of those wily little creatures. Actually, it's rather a long story that I will share with you later. All of us will meet again."

Gretchen and Mary were busy in the farmyard making final preparations. They looked up and saw a great eagle fly over them. As it flew over the farm, a small object fell, and in their thoughts they heard a tiny scream. As it landed, they heard a tiny voice again. "I'm sorry about the scream. That is the farthest I've ever been dropped. Now if you'll excuse me, I have to do my work."

The great raptor flew high above and circled the area until it decided to perch on a tall, standing dead tree that overlooked the small farm. In a flurry of beating wings, the bird landed and began preening her feathers. They then heard another voice. "Rest, my Ariel. I need to find a small cart, do you see one?" Gretchen and Mary looked at each other and smiled. "That, my dear, must be the strangest thing I have yet to see on the plains." "I believe, old one, that it is a good sign."

Gretchen was in deep thought as she was humming a song of remembrance and love. As she stood there, she thought of the secluded grove and the dark eyes that looked through the mists. She felt the breeze against her face and blew a quiet kiss to the memory of her love, when suddenly she heard a scream. She ran back to where Mary was standing rigid and pointing toward a log. "What is that creature doing here?" Gretchen put her arm around Mary in reassurance.

"That little white furry beast is none other than Gustav." "And sorry, dear Gustav, I just wasn't expecting such a handsome spelled knight."

There was a flurry of giggles and laughs heard by Mary as she looked around for the source. "Pay no attention to them, brave warrior of the plains. Your description does me justice. We're here to help you and this gallant warrior to rescue your companion." She looked at the ferret and tilted her head one way, then the other. Then she walked up close to the knight and said "I don't see your lips move." Now there was a thunderous roar of laughter, and she did what she does often and sat down quickly. As the laughter died down, she heard the voice of Ariel. "Madam, please excuse our rude behavior, for we have not explained to you how we communicate. We speak through our minds. This was a magic spell given to us by a wonderful good fairy by the name of Elizabeth. We are so glad that we can speak to you and praise you for being such pioneers."

After she had regained her composure, Mary stood up and continued preparing. "Please, Gustav, forgive me for screaming because there are so many little creatures that resemble you on this great plain. Many of them are pests that scamper around our house, our garden, and compete with us. Who are the other beings in this entourage of yours?" Gustav found a higher perch as he stood upon a bench. Mary watched in fascination as he held up the satchel and then pointed to an eagle that flew above them. "The golden eagle is my love, Ariel. Within this satchel, I carry a pumpkin seed we call Orange. Now that we've been introduced, we need to get to the business at hand. We need a cart and horse to pull it."

They appeared to ponder all that had happened; she gazed forlornly into the distance. "I have been speaking to a wily little creature, an eagle, and I hear others. Can you tell me how he's doing up there?" She heard the answer as Gustav spoke. "He is enduring the ordeal up to now. Those rascals have been moved by his resolve to live, and now they are pulling him on a sled."

CHAPTER THIRTY-ONE

MY KINGDOM FOR A HORSE

Mary started looking for the cart, and she found it behind the barn. She called for Gretchen. "You want to see the war horse that I found in the fields?" With a questioning glance, she looked at Mary and asked, "What color is this horse?" "He is a beautiful shade of gray with a white patch on his muzzle. Why do you ask?" Gretchen looked expectantly toward the barn and said, "I lost a horse in battle." She turned to the warrior in her somewhat defensive posture and said, "I found him on the plain. He's mine, and he will remain mine."

Ignoring the comments from this lady of the plains, Gretchen whistled. The horse, unseen, could be heard snorting and generally stomping around his enclosure. Gretchen began to run, calling out his name in great her excitement, "Gray, Gray, is that you?" She saw the animal and walked up slowly. The beautiful horse was prancing, snorting in nervous anticipation as he rose up on his hindquarters in greeting to Gretchen. The tears of joy were flowing freely at this reunion with a friend.

Gretchen looked at Mary and asked, "May I greet your horse?" Mary nodded her head, and they both walked in to the fenced enclosure. He reared up again and called a greeting. The warrior looked at Mary, shouting, "He is my Gray." The old one was also petting this great beast as she buried her face in his neck. Gretchen then mounted the horse bareback, and the two bolted through the gate of the enclosure. Mary was laughing and crying. As the dynamic couple charged through in a thunder of hooves, the mighty team reached the edge of the forest within minutes. Then they turned and walked back to Mary.

Mary held her hands to her face, smiling, laughing, and enjoying the fruits of her scavenging. The warrior then remounted Gray and demonstrated a high-stepping dance. The duo stopped. And with a whispered command, the tall gray stallion bowed to his mistress with his right leg extended. Gretchen then asked Mary, "Would you care to race the wind?"

Mary laughed when she responded, "Oh my, could I?" Gretchen pulled her up on the side of the horse, and Mary embraced her. With a slight kick, the trio galloped throughout the countryside and even to the top of some of the small hills. Mary was heard hooting and hollering with joy as the thundering hooves carried them around the farm.

Breathless, they dismounted, and then Mary looked at Gretchen. "It is time to get back to business." They were told where to bring the cart, and then they noticed the green sprout bursting from the ground. The pumpkin, whose distant relative had been spelled by a good witch, was now beginning to grow again in size. One could see the small orange-colored orb as it appeared in the center of the cart. Then all watched, and they were mesmerized as vines began extending from the pumpkin and began examining the cart. The pumpkin then thoughtfully asked the question, "Gustav, my old friend, is Ariel about?"

Gustav, looking high above, answered, "I believe that she is very near." He noticed the large bird circling overhead, and now she appeared to be heading down toward the cart. They heard her thoughts. "I'm just overhead, you sweet, dear delicacy." With those thoughtful words, the slithering vines drew back and sought cover. Now spoke the seed in a somewhat whining manner, "There you are, Ariel, are we still friends?" The golden raptor continued down and with a flurry of wings landed and stood on the pumpkin. As she stood there in all her beauty, the great talons were now embedded deep in the soft exterior. "Of course we are friends, my magical fruit of immense evolution." They all heard him cry out, "Ouch, your loving embrace has not changed. Please be gentle." She sniggered. "Was my gentle touch too much?" Then they heard Gustav. "Let us dispense with this silliness and rescue the knight." They all agreed, and the orange orb began his magic.

The vines of the orb began to tighten and secure its purchase of the cart. As Orange expanded, the vines would lengthen and tighten until the pumpkin had grown as high as an average man. There was a flurry of activity, and as it finished, all rested. "That's almost as fast as the last time I grew." The ferret patted the pumpkin and thought for all to hear, "You've done very well. You will be different and a smaller version of your ancestor." "Thank you, Gustav. All of our adventures are still within my memory. Especially emblazoned upon my pumpkin soul was the storming of Elena's castle. Speaking of blazing, all of my friends were sad upon my finish. It seems like that's the only way we get together, but what a meeting."

Gustav was thoughtful for a few moments, and then he said, "The ultimate sacrifices of many thousands have protected countries, ended civilizations, and can have a profound effect on all of us." Mary looked at the pumpkin mounted on her cart and looked above at the eagle. She then turned to the ferret knight as he stood atop the strange carriage. She walked up to him, saying, "I appreciate all of these stories, but our story is now. Those ruffians who have captured my mate will not scare easily. We must be quick to bring out my man. Mr. Pumpkin, it will be very hard riding atop your roundness. Where is our seat?" The orange-colored fruit demonstrated a very happy continence as he asked, "Bring up the horse. I will attach myself to your noble steed. When you are ready, I will create needed seats, and we will be off to the hunt."

CHAPTER THIRTY-TWO

THE CARRIAGE

Gustav thought to himself and, with his tiny, ferret laugh, told everyone, "I have a chant." Mary just shook her head and sighed. "Please be quick with it, little white knight of magic." "Here it goes," said he.

"Round and round the wheels they will go,
A rescue we're on, let us hunt for the foe,
Storm the tall gates, let them know that we're here,
Let the knight know, let us shout a big cheer,
It is Time to assemble, sound the great horn,
Return the wheeled Knight to his wife who be torn,
It's time to charge that ruffian foe,
Doing good for a friend through the Valley we go,
Embrace our grand lives and sip nectar sweet,
In the next orange life, we'll all gladly meet."

They all cheered such a gallant charge. Mary and Gretchen brought the gray horse to stand near the cart. It was then brought to the front of the strange carriage. They stood comforting the horse as the vines found it and formed a harness with reins. "Where are the seats, orb?" Suddenly, they saw indentations in the sides and on top. "I am ready when you are, ladies." Gretchen helped the old one up and then followed. "Shall we be on our way?" They hollered and cheered as they moved forward. The gray horse snorted and shook his head in apparent agreement, and slowly, he picked up speed.

As they sat side by side atop the carriage, they began to pick up speed. It appeared to be a nerve-wracking experience. The old one held tight to the warrior seated next to her, but she began to shout and scream until she hollered, "Stop!" Gretchen pulled hard on the slender reins, and the horse stopped quickly. It happened so quickly that they both were thrown forward. They were quickly embraced by vines that held them, and they were returned to their seats. Mary sat there with eyes wide with horror. Her mouth was dry and parched as she tried to yell out, but all she could do was a raspy bark. "Help, help," she whispered.

Gretchen wrapped her arms around the scavenger and whispered, "Mary, Mary, it is okay." She looked around to the carriage, her horse, and then began a very nervous cackling laugh. "That was my first ride on a pumpkin, surrounded by snakes, I mean wrapped in vines." They felt their seats readjust and the indentations became deeper. "Please forgive me. It has been a while since I have become a carriage." They all heard the ferret knight. "I would say that you all responded very well. Let us be on our way. The dust of those warriors can be seen in the distance." Indeed, Karl and his partners were making better time now that Alan was attached to a sled.

As they continued on their way, the ground was bumpy, full of small and large rocks, but the orb seemed to cushion the ride. "I am just an old mother of the desert, trying to find my husband," said the scavenger and wife. As Gretchen directed the horse, she commented, "Old is an attitude, Mary. Your attitude is one of youthful vigor and a great love of life. Let us find your love and return to your Eden." In response, the old one smiled with a twinkle in her eyes and nodded. She had found her horned helmet and put it on. What a sight she was.

As Gretchen and Mary pursued the kidnappers, Alan was entering the village of Karl and his people. This clan had established this camp over years of travel. It was not permanent, as they were always searching for new food sources. They always appeared to be pursued by starvation and disease. It was located in a small valley. There were forests nearby, which provided tall logs which were roped together to provide a crude wall of protection.

CHAPTER THIRTY-THREE

THE VILLAGE

The small homes were unusual. Some were simple tents of animal skins; others had log walls with tented roofs. Karl was their leader now; fortunately this was a good year for the group. Their young appeared healthy as they ran around the group entering their village. All within the group began to surround them. They all began to focus on Alan upon the sled. Talking to each other, their conversation almost appeared heated as they pointed at Alan and then to Karl. His chair was placed on the ground. As he began to push it around the grounds, the dogs barked and chased him along with the children.

Alan had stopped for a moment to rest and noticed a white-haired woman walking toward him. She said not a word, slowly approaching him. Walking around him, the woman then embraced him. Then, backing away, she cried out, "Shawn, Shawn?" Looking closely at him, she gently touched his face with her long callused fingers and then began to cry. "You're not my Shawn. Where's my boy?" Another villager walked up to her and embraced the woman. She whispered something to her and began walking away. As she walked away, the lady kept looking back and whispering, "Shawn, my Shawn, where are you?"

Karl walked up to Alan, and together they watched and felt the turmoil, emotion, and love lost. "As you entered my village, I saw and felt the memories of those lost in combat. Brothers, sisters, mothers, and fathers all watched you as a living warrior of past battle." There were no loud exclamations of grief or mourning that had passed. There were just quiet tears flowing freely as friends and family embraced, and all sought Alan and his strange wheeled chair.

The native Karl and Alan the wheeled knight conversed as he tried to explain his feelings. "There's a definite contradiction of me being alive and those in your clan who have not returned. Sweet Mary is the answer. She found me, saw to my wounds, and wouldn't let me die. She found a way for me to be productive in our small family. It took many months to construct this chair. Once the chair was made, there were many hours spent falling off the chair and climbing back into it.

CHAPTER THIRTY-FOUR

THE VISION

"Gradually, we realized that our farm needed to be prepared for me. Together, Mary and I cleared pathways, removed obstacles, and built the first of many bridges that span the many gullies and washes that intersect our farm. The winds of mourning still mock me and see me when I am upon the plain. Obstacles remain: immense cliffs rise to stop me, gullies remain uncovered, and the earth is constantly changing from the natural shaping of winds, rains, and man.

"Once," said Alan, "I had propelled myself many miles from our home. I kept pushing myself on until I reached the place that I had never seen. I came to immense canyon of breathtaking beauty, sheer walls, and they called to me. The winds were howling, and a song seemed to place me in. I rolled forward, inch by inch, until I stood on the top of a rock face hundreds of feet high, and within me the voice said that I could fly.

"The immensity of the canyon spelled me as I looked up to the sky. I saw a bird of prey circling high overhead, and I closed my eyes. I called to it and asked it to teach me to fly. In seemingly as a response to my plea, it began a steep dive with screeching cry and speed that was incredible. My eyes were still closed, but I saw the bird land with its wings in slow motion, and I felt the breeze. I also felt its talons dig deep into the muscles of raised arms. The pain was sharp as I began to sleep and my dream continued.

"I began to dream as I became the hawk. My vision was clear to me, as I could now see bushes, small animals in hiding, and details of life stood out to me. I launched to the skies and became the bird in flight. His wings were mine as they began to pull against the wind. My talons were folded next to my body, and I began to reach for the clouds. The speed of my ascent appeared slow as I climbed through the flawless sky.

"I perceived all that was below me and saw my body. Sitting on this chair, perched precariously on the cliff's edge. I then noticed that as I was in my chair, I began to rock back and forth. The forward motion was increasing, and fear coursed through me as I watched myself fall toward the abyss. I then became the man in the chair and witnessed the descent. The winds screamed as I closed my eyes in fear of falling. The winds were whispering as I repeatedly pounded the center of my chest. My vision had ended; I heard a call and awoke.

"I have been touched by a strong dream. The cliff's edge was not the answer, for my purpose and destiny would have to be found. Today, the puzzle continues, but my path becomes clearer." He looked the warrior and said, "A frightful question arises: if we are to save man from the mourning winds, who do we save and who do we leave?" Karl shrugged his shoulders and looked out at his people. "We leave no one behind." Alan nodded his head in agreement and looked out at this people. Alan then commented, "Let us make preparations for my contest in battle. Another solution may come to us through my hissing goose."

The warrior laughed and then stared at the visitor. "We are warrior clan, and contests to take our minds away from our day-to-day lives. Today we are fed, our dwellings stop the rain, and the howling of scavengers is not heard. We're not to fear tomorrow until the sunrise and they have surrounded. Then there will be enough to worry us." Preparations were made as the clan of warriors and their families set in motion the great confrontation. But as this was being done, threatening clouds of trial would soon intimidate all.

Preparations were made as the clan of warriors and families set in motion the great confrontation between the wheeled knight and their leader, Karl. His tenure had depended on the weather, success in battle, and his quickness of intellect. All of which would be put to the test sooner than patent, as other forces were at work, and a trial would soon intimidate all within this story.

CHAPTER THIRTY-FIVE

LESSONS OF LIFE

As Gretchen, Mary, and the orb stopped for the night, the warrior told them that there would be no fire tonight. "I will be first watch, after a brief meal. You all must rest." Mary found warm blankets and slept on the pumpkin. It had provided a larger depression to act as a sleeping place for both ladies. The pumpkin listened to the sounds of the night. It heard the far-off flight of its winged friend with the ferret knight. The words of love between two bewitched souls were heard by the seed.

"They sleep in preparation for our tomorrow." This said by the white ferret to his winged love. "The stars above kindle my love for you, dear Gustav." A rising moon silhouetted the duo as a perch was found above where Alan slept. Soon, all were sleeping lightly, with dreams of lost loves and found adventure.

The next morning found the clan beginning to relax as they were becoming accustomed to Alan. As he rolled through the village, many of the clan would walk up to him and touch him as a talisman. Others would simply nod their head in greeting. Warriors would touch the chair before their scouting party was leaving. Widows would watch and then turn away when observed. The clan began to turn into itself as the old ones were helped more often, and all were more protective of each other.

Living with this sweet Mary had spared him the rigors of communal life. Alan was impressed with this new spirit this seemed to have taken over the village. He continued to practice the crossbow and a short sword. Several of the warriors had volunteered to assist in retrieving bolts and setting up new targets for practice. They were all amazed at the crossbow in its accuracy at short range. They were more aware of the need for removing obstacles from the pathways throughout the village. The village was becoming cleaner than it ever been, and it was becoming more of family.

As Gustav and Ariel watched, he commented, "He doesn't appear to be a prisoner." Alan could be seen practicing out of the village. Karl walked up to him as he continued to practice. "You are a strange man. You've kept your word and now practice for our contest of skill. This contest often results in death or injury to one or both of us, yet you show no fear. I watch as members of the village will touch you, as for good luck. They fear me, follow my commands and leadership. Sometimes, they cower at my anger. They never touch me for good luck. You, strange fellow, have another purpose. What is it?"

"I am not sure, Karl. But I think we will find out soon." As they were conversing, a rider came into view, and all watched as he was whipping his pony with a frenzied effort. There were many shouts as he entered the village. Several of the village caught him as he fainted and slumped off his mount. As he was gently placed on the ground, he was revived. He looked around and called out for his leader. He saw Karl and then breathlessly exclaimed, "The horde, the horde, it comes to devour us. All is lost."

All sounds of the village ceased with those words. They surrounded Karl and the rider, with many of the women softly crying. "They never come this way. Are you sure, my son?" The young rider looked up to his father. "I saw a large dust cloud and thought it a storm. As it approached, I began to see outriders as they scouted for game and whatever was edible. They are a three days' ride from us." Karl embraced his son and then asked, "Tell us everything you saw."

"I watched from a prominent hill as riders scouted. Then I saw the mass of people come into view. The scouts are like the eyes and ears of the body. They are the main defense. I saw fierce warriors mounted and some on foot. Within the perimeter, I saw crude wagons and carts being pulled by their women. There were old ones and young children. All appeared haggard and dirty. It was as a plague sweeping across the plain. No tree, plant, or living thing was left as they cut a wide swath through the land. They all appeared hungry as this mass approaches us." The rider again slumped upon the ground in fitful sleep.

CHAPTER THIRTY-SIX

THE HORDE

The duo above had heard the news, as Gustav said, "We must speak to Alan, now." They went lower, and soon Alan was startled by Gustav's voice. "Alan, you are in grave peril. What is your relationship with these warriors?" He responded, "They are friendly, and we all are in trouble." As Ariel flew in wide circles above the camp, Alan continued the conversation. "Please persuade my Mary and the warrior to leave as quickly as possible." Gustav answered, "Dear fellow, you know that mate of yours will not change her mind. You, the warrior, and I must come up with a plan to divert this mass of humanity away to other pastures."

Karl watched and wondered of the lunacy of his captive. He watched Alan as he gestured wildly and appeared to speak to the sky. As Karl looked around, he noticed the people of the village as they became more animated at watching the wheeled knight. He motioned all for silence, and he quietly walked up to Alan. He appeared to consider striking the knight, but instead he placed his right hand on Alan's shoulder and shook him gently. Alan was startled as he looked to Karl and then around to the villagers. "May I help you, Karl?"

"Crazy man who speaks to invisible beings or to himself, my villagers are becoming alarmed at not being included in this conversation. Tell us of anything that will help us face the horde." "I am so sorry that I have not included you in this most important subject. Karl, close your eyes, and may I introduce you to Gustav and his love, Ariel." The bronzed warrior, still questioning, peeked through his closed eyes. He saw no one, but he heard the voice. "Leader of a strong clan, I am most honored to speak with you."

Suddenly, Karl turned wide eyed to those surrounding him and covered his mouth. "Who or what is a Gustav?" There was silence for a moment, then again he heard, "I was a swordsman and knight of a realm many days' travel from here. I and my love were spelled into small beasts. There was a good spell given to balance the bad, and that is our ability to speak through our minds."

With the word, "beast," Karl stepped back and reached for his knife. He looked around in fear but quickly took a deep breath and called to his people. "It is okay. Let me think, and I will find solutions to our adversary." All had seen him reach for his weapon, and they followed in like manner. They lowered their weapons and slowly formed a human chain around their leader. Facing outward, they awaited his words.

"Your village follows you well. They show signs of great training and trust." As he began to relax, still covering his mouth, he spoke, "They know me and can sense when I am alarmed or in need of their presence. We are family, and we must be this way to survive. Now, beast, where do we go from here to save my family and yours?"

They felt soft breezes that whispered to them, and all heard the howls of a lone wolf. It was a strange and mournful call as all looked in its direction. Alan smiled and looked up to Karl. "I believe that you are hearing a female or two." Karl looked at him and with a woeful smile asked, "More of your friends, I presume." He nodded and looked out. "Friends, yes, and also we could be hearing the winds of battle. These breezes often sigh with challenges to me in my quest of survival. Since my love brought me back to life and gave me a will to live, their haunting, laughing calls offer insults on my darker days."

A little child interrupted them. Karl knelt down and embraced her. He stood, holding her, and spoke. "The strangeness of these days tax my mind and abilities. I speak to an invisible beast who seeks to save my village. I capture a knight on a wheeled chair—he now appears to be my advisor. Peculiar are these days."

Karl put the little one down and then looked up to the cloud. "Beast?" "Gustav, I am at your service, warrior." He looked around to the villagers who watched. "Can you quickly scout out the horde and report to me what we must do to save us all." "I rise with the wind, and we will fly to meet this moving devourer of humanity. We will find new paths for it to take."

With a questioning glance around, he thought, *Fly?* "Fly we will in the winds of change to save your small kingdom." Karl looked at the departing raptor and asked, "You are the great golden eagle?" "That, my friend, is my partner, my love, and my transport. We will do whatever it takes. Adieu."

As Gustav felt the winds, he held tight to his winged love. "This is probably our most dangerous travel. Thank you for your flight and your feathered love." She giggled as he embraced her, and together they sought the horde. A short distance away from Karl's village rode Mary and Gretchen. The gray horse pulling the pumpkin carriage demonstrated a slow trot. The path was rock strewn, which accounted for the carriage swerving and bouncing at times. Gretchen often looked down at the face of the carriage. "Your handsome face registers some discomfort, orange orb?" She heard a thoughtful shout. "Indeed, warrior, driver, and punisher." Gretchen had to laugh as she pondered where she was and to whom she was speaking.

The carriage halted just below the crest of a hill, and wrapped in the vines' embrace, Mary whispered, "Let me out of here, you orange beast. I must see to my personal needs. I also cannot feel my legs." Telepathically, they all heard him sigh. "I have halted, my lady. I too have things to do, including an inventory of my parts. I think I am missing a few things." The carriage was showing cracks and holes in its body. Gretchen cautiously crept to the crest of the hill and observed the village in the distance.

Mary had finished her "business" and now stood at the warrior's side. Mary gasped and put her hand to her mouth to silence herself. She pointed beyond the village, and all saw the distant, rolling dark cloud. "There, my friend, is the signature cloud of the horde." As Mary looked down into the village and saw her mate, she began waving and hooting. Gretchen shook her head at her partner and said, "Well, I guess it is time for an entrance."

Before they began their entrance, Gretchen put on her sculptured helmet, tied the shield to her mount with her broadsword. The warrior's helmet was a beautiful metal form of a woman's face. There were the standard eye slits and a slit in back to accommodate her braid. The broadsword was made of a very strong light metal and seemed to sing when it performed its terrible work. Mary, on the other hand, was wearing her leather helmet with deer horns.

Gretchen was astride the gray mount. Mary was seated within a seat within the pumpkin. As they approached the village, one could only see the top of her helmet. Small children began running to their parents, old ones gasped, and their leader stood there with arms folded. "A warrior on horseback, pulling an immense pumpkin with a small but fierce-looking woman hidden inside. This must be your mate, Alan?" Karl winced as he heard the telepathic voice again. "These are friends, and we all are here to help your village." As he heard this, he saw the old one encased within the orb jump out and run toward her mate. She almost knocked him over as she jumped in his lap. While she embraced him, whispered words of endearment were given, which ended with a very passionate kiss.

All averted their eyes, and many smiled at the emotional reunion. The wheeled knight appeared to enjoy the passion, but he also tried to calm her. "My hissing goose, we will have time for more of this when we survive the coming ordeal. One or two more sweet kisses, and then we must all plan our survival." After a long, lingering final kiss, the small microcosm of humanity turned toward the threatening cloud. Karl looked at Gretchen and smiled slightly. He talked aloud, "Tell us, beast, where are they, and do we have a chance to save ourselves?"

Gustav spoke slowly for all to receive his thoughts. "There is always a chance for survival. Our problems are the outriders. We must direct them away from your valley. The horde is hungry, and that is why they move. They are watching us as we speak." Gretchen had dismounted and was checking Gray. As they were listening and pondering their fate, Karl walked up to her. Their eyes met; she saluted and bowed slightly. "I am Gretchen of Angus Castle." He blushed slightly saying, "A maiden warrior to the rescue, No one will believe my story." She smiled saying, "We'll just have to keep it among ourselves." She then laughed.

There was a mutual attraction as she spoke. "I was a farm girl who was trained in secret by my uncle. My family told me to leave, as they were embarrassed by my decision. After this, I survived by my wits and finally was able to join King Angus's militia. Now I am on a quest with magical beings, including this cart. Mary, the scavenger, Gustav, Ariel, and the seed stand ready. Orange, the seed, is especially ready with a long history of service and mayhem."

The tiny voice was heard by all as a whiny shout. "Mayhem! I'll have you know that it wasn't my fault." Karl shrugged his shoulders and whispered, "Another of your strange voices?" He now heard a tiny giggle. "Yes, great leader, it is I, the pumpkin upon the cart who accompanies these noble servants." He turned to the pumpkin upon the carriage and thought he saw a face upon the orb. "Welcome," said the leader of the village, "but please, no other magic moments."

They all agreed. Above the village, Gustav and Ariel said goodbye and turned toward the threatening cloud. "My ferret love, this is an adventure like nothing we've experienced. There is more danger, more people in danger, than we have ever seen. You and I must be cautious in our pursuit of the horde." Gustav embraced the great feathered raptor and held his tiny head close to her. "We will make a difference, my love. Whatever it takes, we will do it." All those below who heard this exchange shouted out, "Whatever it takes, we will be there." This was repeated by the villagers as Karl turned to them and held up his arms in response.

Later in the afternoon, Gretchen found a moment to speak with Karl. "I have yet to know your name, sir." As they had found a secluded area, the two warriors sat next to each other, and he began to speak. "It may seem strange to you, but I took this name from a warrior who had shown great battle strength. I was sorry that our battle ended with his death. Honoring him, I took his name. I am Karl."

CHAPTER THIRTY-SEVEN

TO MEET AN ENEMY

Gretchen's face flushed, and without thinking, she rose and drew her sword. "My Karl? You defeated my Karl? The only one I ever loved?" She had drawn her weapon, and with both hands on the hilt of her sword, she thrust the blade into the ground and knelt next to it and cried. The warrior named Karl backed away, quieting the villagers. He waited. "Oh, the futility of war," she cried and then looked up to Karl's namesake. She then smiled, then laughed and cried out, "He would have loved to seen this reunion. That was the kind of man he was."

Even with this strange turn of events, preparations were being made for possible war. High above, the high-flying duo proceeded to search out the marauding mass of humanity. "There," thought Gustav, as they both saw two scouts turning their mounts and beginning a wild gallop away from the village. "We must fly close to them and listen." "I agree," said the raptor. The voices were heard. "That village will feed many." This said by one of the tanned, muscular riders. The two men wore animal skins and sat astride very fast ponies. Their legs were clamped tight to the sides of the panting multicolored horses. They moved like the wind, as both embraced the necks of their steeds. The young boys kept looking back, as their long black hair flowed as a greeting to their pursuers. "That eagle appears to be following us. Do you think it is a good omen?"

"If it is a watchful spirit of that place, we are doomed." One rider brought his pony to a quick stop, turned, and notched an arrow. "I will not run like an old woman." It was a well-aimed shot as the long feathered missile hunted the magical duo. "Oh, be careful, my love," Gustav said as he saw the shaft approach. Time appeared to slow as Ariel turned slightly away from the projectile; Gustav hung on to the strong cord as now he appeared to be flying. In an instant, the golden eagle grabbed it and somehow snapped it into two pieces. The riders watched as the broken pieces floated through the air, gradually landing peacefully on the ground.

They screamed a warrior's call, turned their panting horses and began to ride as men crazed with fear. Their mounts responded to the urgency with incredible ground-leaping strides. Then the leader heard a small voice pierce his soul. "Chan, please listen, and do not fear." Looking wildly around, even to his fellow riders, he asked, "Who speaks to me of fear?" He shook his head as both riders had heard the voice. Their horses were now whipped into a foaming frenzy as they looked ahead at their protective cloud. "You cannot leave us those easy young riders."

"We will meet you in battle, strange one. Our children and women spend many sleepless nights hungry. The warriors anguish as they hear their famished calls. We are many in the family, and we can overcome your magic." Ariel had found a perch on top a nearby cliff as Gustav spoke. "Do not flee like frightened old men. Let us talk." The warrior Chan brought his horse to an abrupt stop and dismounted. He stood shaking with the thrill of the chase; he turned and began looking to the sky. The other rider sat upon his mount and watched, listening to his partner. Chan tore off his shirt and withdrew his long knife. He then shouted out for all to hear, "Take me now or later in battle. Either way, I will do whatever it takes to feed my people." "You are a brave and formidable soldier. If all are like you, we could be doomed," this said by the ferret knight.

His pony had not moved from where he stopped. Quickly, the young member of the marauding horde quickly jumped on top of the animal. "I must return to my people. My children are hungry, and if I don't discover food, they will find a new leader. Whatever solutions you may find, be careful as you approach us. If you get too close, there will be many arrows to dodge, and you may be taken from the skies. We will meet again." Gustav and Ariel watched as the dust of the riders led toward the darkness that was headed their way.

Back at the village, Mary sat within the arms of her Alan. She smiled, turned, and looked into his face, saying, "It was worth the ride in the pumpkin to be reunited with you, my cackling hen." With a peck on the cheek and somewhat out of character, the scavenger grasped Alan's arm and snuggled close to his side, appearing to shiver. He looked at her as her silver hair waved in the breeze. He kissed her gently. Mary then straightened up in her seat and turned toward Gretchen, saying, "Sister, we are ready to help turn the tide."

CHAPTER THIRTY-EIGHT

TO MEET AND LOVE

Gretchen had been in quiet conversation with Karl as she heard Mary's comment. She turned and looked down to her, and her face appeared flushed. Looking at Mary, she winked and then, turning to the head of the village, said, "Great warrior, I and my motley squad are available to assist you in distracting the crowd of humanity. We will change their direction."

"Ah, yes. Distractions. We must strike quickly and with force. The horde will possibly seek other less stressful directions. Hopefully the tide will turn." This said by the warrior as she and Karl walked together as preparations were beginning. "I worry for my village, as all of these strange happenings appear to have struck the heart of these people. First, we have the wheeled knight and then the tumultuous arrival of you, the scavenger, and the strange orange carriage you pulled. If that wasn't enough, there is a winged knight who warns me of the horde.

Now here I stand with a beautiful warrior whom I am sending off to battle a monstrous collection of hungry people. You, Gretchen, I pray will return and meet with me again." He patted her shoulder. She raised the visor on her helmet and smiled. "We will meet again." All in the vicinity watched in fascination as she pulled off her helmet, pulled him to her in a mutual embrace, and then they kissed. There was a collective call of oohhs and ahhhs. Everyone then turned their backs and allowed the couple a few moments of respite before the confrontation.

Mary stood before the village elders, and within her hand was a long branch. She drew a rough map of the area and began to describe her idea. "On the high plateaus, there are great herds of smelly horned beasts. They feed on the grass. As I said, they are huge, smelly brutes that could be a plentiful supply of meat and skins. If people are careful not to take more than is needed, this source could provide food for many years. If we can move part of these animals down this canyon, we could use them as a lure for the horde." One of the villagers shouted, "I'd rather be captured by the horde than try to move one of those terrible things. They have a worse temperament than my mate's clan."

After a very quiet moment, the whole village began to laugh and hoot. It broke their fear for a moment. Gretchen spoke again. "Karl, we must move quickly if this is to be accomplished. I believe with my horse and I pulling Mary in the carriage, we could herd and divide the beasts." Then they heard Alan speak as he sat in his chair next to his mate in the pumpkin. "If the pumpkin will make room, I wish to sit next to my hissing goose." "One more for transport, a simple task, and I am at your service." Alan found a seat next to her as several of the men helped him to his seat, and all were ready.

"Stop," called the warrior chief. "You will not do this alone. I will help, and I'll ask for volunteers from the village. You, lovely warrior, will not face this without me at your side." There were again wild hoots from the crowd until he turned to them with a frown. They quieted until he smiled and gave a quick wink. Gustav was heard. "We must find the herd soon, before nightfall. We must be quiet and not spook them, or all will be lost." The mysterious vines had encircled Alan in a careful embrace. Gretchen's mount began to pull them forward. "I believe Gray is up to the task. Be ready for a ride." The wheeled cart was hidden away in a secure place as the strange procession began.

All was prepared, and they were ready as Gretchen mounted the great horse, and it danced in its exuberance to run. Mary watched. Mary spoke quietly spoke to Alan. "I remember when I first saw that horse and rider dance. I pray that we will all be safe so we may watch them once more." He squeezed her shoulder, and soon all moving out to engage the horde in a dangerous game. The rider of the golden eagle flew above. "You may notice a different cloud a distance away from the horde. That is our herd." The great bird and the ferret knight banked and headed toward a solution. "It appears as the horde has stopped for the night. We have just one night to move the beasts before that mass reaches the village."

CHAPTER THIRTY-NINE

MOVE THE HAIRY BEASTS

Within several hours of flying, Gustav saw the beasts, and they found a perch to observe. He heard the voice of Elizabeth, the good fairy. "Good evening to you both. I thought it would help just a little bit. I have listened to the great beasts. They are very difficult to understand. I actually tried speaking to one, and he ran for miles before he stopped. They are very, very temperamental, even more so than my late sister. They live on much grass for grazing. And as I said, they will spook or run at the least amount of surprise.

"So you must have Gretchen and the inhabitants of the orange cart move very slowly within the herd. All thoughts must be directed to Gustav and especially you, Mr. Orange." Gustav spoke to all, and they listened and waited patiently. "Great Orange, the pumpkin of many seasons, you will be led through part of the herd. Remember, they may perceive the pumpkin as food, and they may even be tempted to nibble. "Nibble, am I a worm?" said he with a curious expression.

"Please," the ferret knight pleaded, "remember not to react that way. These wonderful beasts may feel your fear and stampede. Then all will be lost." The passengers within the pumpkin felt what may be perceived as a sigh. "I know that I am expendable, but I've also realized my cargo is precious. I will do whatever it takes to keep them safe. Into the mouth of the beast I go."

Traveling at night was very dangerous, but with Gretchen's sure sight, the beasts were found. There was an overpowering stench of animal as the strange carriage pulled by a beautiful gray horse entered among the herd.

Large dark forms were seen milling about in the moonlight. No one spoke or dared to think. There were several of Karl's men who had accompanied them.

They heard Elizabeth's calming voice. "Please keep your thoughts to a minimum so they will not feel your emotion. When we divide the herd, it must be very subtle. Use your sticks with a very gentle brushing motion. Coach them by brushing their backsides. No sudden moves or shouts as I think of a delicate chant:

Gently blows a nighttime breeze.

Move the beasts, move them, please

Direct them, coach them, move them east.

Let us share the hairy beasts.

The movement was subtle, as slowly the animals began to move and shuffle forward. They moved toward the canyon, but this was accompanied by all sorts of snorting and huffing. It appeared as a rebellion beginning to circulate among the herd. Gently the voice of years and Elizabeth spoke to the great animals. "A quiet walk in the moonlight to greener grass and the lower plain is why you move." They quieted, and all heard the sound of their hooves clumping forward with great weight and sleepiness.

Gretchen gently reached with her branch to brush the backside of the beautiful animals. They all heard her gentle voice in a surprising chant. "You go left, and the next to the right. A help for the horde, we walk through the night. A firm little touch as I move the beast east. Move large, move small, from great to the least." The woman smiled and commented, "It wasn't very good, but it helped."

As they moved, pulling the great pumpkin carriage and its occupants, she gently patted the neck of the great gray horse. It appeared to nod his head as they moved forward. As they moved a portion of the herd, a large male with streaks of gray and scars of battle demonstrating his status appeared to balk. He started to snort, huff, and show his resistance. The herd began to slow down, and some appeared to be turning. The good fairy spoke. "Gretchen, you must speed up gently, as they are sensing the pumpkin's presence."

As the herd was moving at a greater pace, the seed of orange orb spoke. "I have heard them chewing their cud and inhaling the air. Oh my goodness, I've been wounded." Mary and Alan looked back to see a large bite that had been taken from the pumpkin. They saw the snout of one of the hungry beasts, and Mary spoke. "You, Mr. Orange, must pick up the pace, if you wish to continue this journey in one piece." Gretchen coached her mount to move faster as the herd followed. The pace quickened. The trail they were following was illuminated by moonlight. The strange procession snaked its way down from the plateau. The hungry creatures were all motivated by the sweet scent. For their large size, they moved with quickness.

Gustav spoke to all, to the pumpkin, and to its occupants. "I go ahead to prepare the fiery gate to persuade the beasts in their movement." Then they heard a quieter, more subtle voice from the orb. "You, my friends were going to be wrapped within my vines for safety. It will be as a cocoon. You will be safe no matter what happens to me. My sweet Mary, you must take deep, slow breaths and relax. I know the vines make you very nervous. Please be still and know that I am with you."

Mary took a quick breath as the vines began to wrap around her. She closed her eyes and thought of her cackling hen. "I love you, Alan." Alan too was encased in a shell as quietly they waited. The carriage was moving just ahead of the hungry animals. Karl and a few of his warriors were also moving through the herd. It was almost unsettling to them, as they had never tried to mingle with the great beasts.

Gustav and Ariel flew above and ahead of the moving herd. He had never flown at night with her. Now he saw the beauty of the moon as its gentle light illuminated the herd as it descended from the highlands. The plateau stretched many miles and was home to a variety of animals. He saw those that were shepherding the large animals and felt the danger. As the glided in a clear, dark sky, he saw the many campfires of the multitude.

CHAPTER FORTY

TO FEED THE HUNGRY

As they circled above them, he heard the many cries of hungry children. He even felt the hunger pangs of the adults. Listening intently, he found Chan, the leader of these people. "Chan?" he called out to him. "It is you, winged beast . . . Do you hear the cries of my children? Do they not cut through your soul, magical being?" The ferret knight responded, "Indeed, Chan, the call to the depths of our hearts. That is why we are here."

There is a narrow canyon that can act as a trail. It leads down from the plateau. There is a portion of the beasts that is being herded down the canyon. "What are these beasts you speak of?" "They are large, very temperamental beasts that offer large amounts of meat, and their hides are thick and warm. You can help move them as they come down the large ravine. You must build a beacon, a fire to direct the herd into a valley that is left of your families.

"There are villagers who will help you in hunting and processing this bounty. This is a resource that must be carefully managed." "Those are large words from a strange being." Gustav laughed quietly. "I only meant that you hunt only for food, clothing, and that there is no waste." Chan also had a brief moment to sigh. "As you may have noticed, there is no waste from my large family."

Several leaders of the village and the horde met near where the canyon entered the lower plain. Together they built a large bonfire. The flames were reflected by the canyon walls, and within moments the beasts reluctantly were directed into an open valley. Many of the warriors were shocked to see these animals up close. They realized that this was a thundering sustenance that could feed all within their families.

Alan called to Mary, "I feel the rushing of the cart as we are part of this tumult. We are breaking apart, and we may be at the mercy of the beasts. Just know, my dear one, you will always be my hissing goose." Shouting above the noise, Mary called to the magic seed, "You get us out of here, or I will have pumpkin pie until all of your progeny are cooked thoroughly."

CHAPTER FORTY-ONE

SEEKING MY LOVE

They all heard his voice. It was weak, and it increased and then decreased with each bump and rattle. "Do you really think that I would leave you in the path of these brutes? You do not know the great orb. I will tighten your cocoons." Mary and Alan felt the vines begin to shrink. "That's good!" they both shouted. It was a very tight fit, but they were safe.

"Now for the ride of your lives, I am going to eject you from the pumpkin when I find a quiet spot. I see a good spot coming up. I wish you well. On the count of one, two, three, and the two vine-covered humans were shot through the walls of the orb. They landed in a protected area of the valley. The beasts continued to plod past the pods. With the pods' expulsion, the pumpkin began to break up until it disintegrated. They heard the tiny voice. "Gustav, don't forget me. I will see you all again. The herd began to slow as they found water and grass in abundance with bites of sweet pumpkin.

Many surrounded the vine-covered beings. Gretchen shouted, "Open them quickly." They first opened the pod with Mary. She moved and stretched. Moaning briefly, she called out, "Where is he?" They had opened Alan's shell and pulled out the valiant knight. They all looked at each other and then down to Alan. He was not moving. She slowly walked up to where he lay and hollered, "No, you will not leave me. There is too much for this feeble old lady to do." She crawled up to him and felt his brow. He was warm and lay still, not breathing.

"Alan, Sir Alan of the Seven-Year War, awaken. Okay, if you wish to be stubborn, my breath becomes your breath." She breathed into him with a kiss of life. My job is to push you around. Yours is to hold me in your lap on cool nights." She became rougher as she pushed his chest and then breathed. Her tears were now freely flowing as now she was pleading between breaths. "We must watch the morning sun arise and light the sky. Dear old cackling hen, Feel life and live." With one more breath, she fell on his chest and cried with the mourning winds. The others felt this love of the scavenger of the plain, the anguish washed over them, and many wept openly. Then, all at once, he began coughing and sputtering. "I haven't left yet, quit beating me."

There were strange sounds heard as many were hooting and hollering, which echoed against the ancient hills. The leaders of the horde and Karl of the village were amazed at all the magical events. Then Mary stood between them, wiping her eyes as she looked to both. "These things did have some magic, but it was also determination that brought this finale. I was determined to save my husband. You needed food, and we all needed success. We found it, thanks to all of you." She walked back up the trail and found remnants of the orb. She knelt down and picked up a seed. "How do I thank you, silly magical pumpkin?" She heard several voices. "You have, dear one." In the dim moonlight, she saw an eagle fly over and then appear to pick up a small creature at the top of a large rock. As all watched these events, they knew that they must pass it on through stories to their young.

As this tale ends, it is good to know several happenings. Mary and Alan continued scavenging and farming. They were also good storytellers to those who passed through. Many were shown the wheeled chair and how to build it. The warrior, Gretchen, stayed with Karl's village and became his mate. Chan helped his very large family. They reduced their numbers by creating families of hundreds and fifties, but not until all had skills to hunt and find edible plants.

Gustav and Ariel were showing their years as they rested. As they slept, the good fairy Elizabeth had a visitor. "I am sorry that I have been so wicked, how can I help?" This was spoken by the ghost of her sister. "Well, Catherine, my big sister, how about a dream spell for these lovebirds?" Her wicked sister giggled. "Why, most certainly." Ariel and Gustav dreamed a marvelous dream. They were lying in human form. He felt her, she him, and then they stood and embraced. His face appeared somewhat aged, but she was ageless, as only a beautiful woman should be. Together they walked into a lovely, colorful sunrise, and the dream would continue into the eternities. The loving couple looked around and then, in unison, said, "We will see you later, godmother."